THE NECROMANCER'S DAUGHTER

The Ghostspeaker Chronicles Book 6

PATTY JANSEN

Capricornica Publications

GET FREE EBOOKS

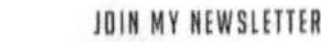

Visit pattyjansen.com
to sign up for Patty's mailing list. You get four series starter
ebooks for free!

CHAPTER 1

I T WAS AT DUSK on a warm summer evening that Queen Johanna of Saarland walked through the palace hallway accompanied by two guards, each carrying an oil lamp to light her way. She had been sitting in the private sitting room when the guards had come to call her. Apparently a visitor had come to the palace. The guards wouldn't say who it was, only that he waited in the garden room.

As she followed the guards across the hall into the large ballroom, where their footsteps echoed in the empty space and the flapping flames of lamps in sconces did weird things with shadows, several scenarios played in Johanna's mind, none of them pleasant.

It could be a representative of the Belaman Church, unhappy with the accusation that they had been trying to control Saardam through a magical relic. That accusation had proven very hard to kill, even if Johanna herself didn't believe there was much truth in it. Yes, the relic had come from the holy city of Seneza and had been sent to the Shepherd Victor, leader of the Church of the Triune in Saardam by someone dressed as a monk, but Johanna refused to believe that the Most Holy Father Severino of the Belaman Church would sanction such a thing. Or if he did, he could not possibly be terribly holy. Which, in itself, would be a scandal of the first order.

It would be better then, that the visitor was someone from Saardam's nobles, who were still sour over their loss of position when King Roald had taken the throne, and more recently, the death of one of their young men. Young Auguste had *fallen* off the deck of a ship where he wasn't supposed to be, and although the nobles wanted to accuse someone of his murder, all the signs showed it had been an unfortunate accident revealing some of the young man's illegal activities. Johanna didn't think the nobles had any reason to accuse, nor draw attention to the young man's activities.

But maybe the visitor was an envoy from any of the guests about to arrive in the city to negotiate potential investment in Saardam's gutted port. They were kings and barons and princes, as well as a slew of folk with commercial interests who would be tagging along.

But it was the first group—the foreign nobles—that had taken Johanna a disproportionate amount of time to deal with. Heaven knew King William had been difficult enough already, almost to the point where Johanna wished he'd declined involvement in the project—and he hadn't even arrived in the city yet.

The start of that meeting was less than a week away. The men and their entourage were about to arrive in Saardam, to gawk, to bicker, and hopefully to agree on a few things or put down sorely needed deposits on sorely needed facilities.

The palace was being readied for that event. For weeks, the palace servants had been run off their feet, building, painting, fixing, cleaning, furnishing.

Already, they had put tables and chairs in place for the

dinners that would be held in the formal ballroom, the hall that Johanna now traversed in the darkness and where the large space echoed her footfalls and those from the guards' hard-heeled boots.

The tablecloths were still in the linen cupboard, safe from the sparrows that lived in the bay window inside the domed roof where no one could reach them and came into the room when the doors were open, and that would leave little reminders of their presence on the pristine white cloth.

The guards led Johanna through the doors to the side of the hall into the garden room. Looking towards the west, the many windows and glass doors of garden room caught the last of daylight, a mere orange glimmer on the horizon.

Every time she came here, a little shiver went over her. This was where she had seen so many men killed during the first attack on Saardam by Alexandre's bandits, and where she had seen the ghost of Princess Celine crack the stone slab in the ground and rise from the grave. The bodies of the soldiers had long since been removed, the broken glass swept up and the headstone replaced, but the foul magic atmosphere lingered as if something had died here and the decomposing juices had seeped into the stone, and could not be removed by any amount of scrubbing.

A single lamp burned in the room, casting a pale yellow glow over the floor and stone that marked Princess Celine's grave. A bench stood there these days, for Johanna came to sit here in the afternoons when the low sun set beyond the wide expanse of the river, behind the marshy shore on the other side and the sand dunes that sheltered Saardam from the force of the sea. She would sit, pray to the holy Triune and contemplate all they had lost and all that needed to be done. It was not a pleasant thing, to come here, but she felt she owed it to Roald's sister and his parents.

Today, someone else sat on that bench.

As Johanna came in, the dark-haired young man turned around and rose at the same time. The orange glow from the flame showed his olive-skinned face with a pair of clear, alert eyes the colour of the night.

His mouth spread into a smile.

"Oh," was all Johanna could say. Her heart jumped.

She hadn't seen Li Fai for over two months, had been avoiding him because . . . because that subtle, polite smile ignited a warm feeling in her that reminded her of all the reasons why she was avoiding him.

And by the Triune, she understood *why* she was avoiding him: because in his quiet, unassuming way, he was heart-stoppingly handsome.

He wore locally made clothes that were classy because of their understated simplicity. No excessive frills on the collar, no garish patterns on the trousers. He'd also done away with the jacket and wore only a plain waistcoat. It was warm enough.

"You look . . . different," he said.

"What, this?" She put her hand on her swollen stomach. It had grown very big and round. She would joke that her dress could double as an army tent. At any rate, she had said goodbye to her toes and would not be able to see them until after the child was born. Still a month to go, Helena said. Just enough time to get these meetings with kings and barons and dukes over and done with.

Li Fai said, "I haven't seen you for so long. I wanted to teach some magic, but you are always busy."

"I'm sorry. I have a lot of work to do. The city is in a big mess." She was such a liar.

"I understand." He looked down. The light gilded his face, the skin soft and smooth. He was about as tall as she.

A little uncomfortable silence followed, in which she

would have liked to say something about how much she enjoyed learning about magic and hearing the stories about the "art" boxes that children in his country received if they had any magic capability. But she couldn't say that because the guard stood behind her, and she was unsure how much the guards knew about magic, or how much they knew about all the other things that had gone on in the Shepherd's house or before.

And the silence was painful because she didn't *want* it to be so awkward and uncomfortable. She wanted to talk and laugh, and practice magic.

She finally found something to say. "I still . . . have the box." Her cheeks glowed. "I keep it on the shelf in my study."

"Do you open it?"

"Sometimes, when no one is looking. The tree grows in it every time." That tree had saved her life when facing the ancient relic sent by the church.

Li Fai smiled again, and that smile almost made her cry. If life was simple, if she had been ordinary Johanna Brouwer, living with her father and being reminded that she should get married, she might have smiled back, and batted her eyelids. She might have hoped that he would ask her to come and visit his family at the iron ship, or go for a walk along the canals.

But she was the king's wife, even if the king was far more interested in frogs than ruling the country, and life was altogether far more complicated.

And she really had no time for this kind of nonsense. She should stay distant and royal, like a real queen. "Do tell me why you have come to see me."

"I'm very sorry about the time of day. This is a quite disturbing matter, though."

"Please sit down."

He sat on the bench.

Johanna hesitated, but the bench had a soft comfortable cushion. Her legs tended to hurt when standing too long, so she sat carefully, at the very far end of the bench, so as not to give that guard whose name she didn't know—where had he gone anyway?—a reason to raise his eyebrows.

Only then did she notice the plain cloth bag that lay on the seat next to him.

He picked it up and inserted his hand into the cloth.

He extracted an object consisting of a dark wooden hand-grip with a metal tube that reflected the light from the lamp.

"Is this. . . ?"

"A gun, yes."

She had seen powder guns before. Johan Delacoeur, a military man, scoffed at guns. He always said that he could do so much more with ten good archers and swordsmen than with twenty men with guns. But clearly, inventors improved the weapons all the time, and this didn't look like any kind of gun she had seen. Those had been awkward things with long barrels that had a little lever at the back that contained a burning match. Johan said that the smell of the burning match gave away the position of a marksman.

This weapon's barrel was quite short. It had a little metal lever on top, but was otherwise smooth.

Li Fai turned it over. Embossed in the wood was a little sign. He held it up to the light and Johanna could make out the dragon symbol that his father, the eastern merchant Li Han, used to mark goods sold through his company.

"Your father's?"

Li Fai shook his head. "There are twelve of these, all of them with our stamp. Or something that looks like our stamp. We didn't put it there. This weapon is not bad, but not of a quality that my father would consider selling."

Only then did she fully comprehend what he was telling her: even after they had unmasked the lame efforts by Auguste LaFontaine, someone was still smuggling.

"How can that be?" The group of Auguste LaFontaine and his friends had been unmasked, their fake stamps taken away, and any goods confiscated. There hadn't been that much to begin with. It had been, Anton of the guards had assured her, a very amateur operation.

She met Li Fai's eyes. "Where did you find this?"

"We didn't. The harbourmaster's diligent staff found it. Since we found those other falsified stamps, they have been looking out for this sort of thing."

"Where did they find it?"

"Packed into crates being unloaded from a Burovian ship that arrived from Florisheim. The captain says he's just carrying stock and doesn't know anything about it."

"Do you believe him?"

Li Fai shrugged. "It's bad form to open cargo that you're contracted to carry." Which wasn't really an answer. It was, however, how the Church relic had made it to Saardam on board Li Han's ship. To a captain, honour was often more important than law. Even if you knew that cargo might be illegal, you did not open crates and look in bags, if you wanted repeat business and if you wanted to keep your good name.

"Yes, but he should have found it suspicious, with this shipment coming from Florisheim with your stamp already on it. The crates would have had your stamp, too."

"They did, and the captain still may not have had any reason to question it." He sounded like *he* would have questioned it. It sounded like he would not have carried the freight without a good explanation. "He *should* have questioned it. I believe that if the captain or the guards had the wood art, they would have seen why they shouldn't have carried it."

Ah. There was the reason that he had come. Li Fai, of course, *didn't* see things in wood. She reached out for the wooden handgrip of the gun.

"Not that one. It has been handled by too many people in the last few days."

He put his hand back into the bag and retrieved a piece of wood. It was a splintered piece the length of her hand. The wood was roughly cut and unpolished.

"I took this from the crate's lid. I had to be quite forceful with the wood to remove it, but I didn't touch it with my hands."

Johanna took it from him. The moment her hands came into contact with the rough wood, her mind filled with images.

Li Fai swinging an axe. It hit the wood with a giant thunk. Ouch.

Then two guards carrying the crate. One of them was complaining about how heavy it was.

The crate sat on a table in the harbourmaster's office. Li Fai stood over it, looking, wide-eyed at its contents.

Then a much vaguer scene. It was dark, and two men were carrying the crate up an incline that was possibly the ladder out of a ship's hold. They spoke in rough, foreign voices. Another man met them on the deck, also speaking in a foreign language, possibly Burovian. The men set the crate at the man's feet. He wore a dark cloak and boots with silver buckles. This man looked like a noble.

He argued with the ship's captain. Johanna had taken some lessons in Burovian, and she thought she heard the word for *payment*. Was the noble taking the crate off the ship? Was he delivering it? Buying it?

Then the arguing men suddenly fell quiet. The two men

who had carried the crate hid behind a stack of different crates. The noble scurried down a little set of stairs into the door to the ship's cabin.

On the quay, someone shouted in the darkness, "Halt. Who goes there?"

No one replied.

Then the images faded.

Johanna again faced Li Fai in the darkness of the garden room, the expression on his face eager. She shook her head. "I can't tell. Too much has happened since for the memories to still be clear enough to identify people."

Disappointment showed in his face.

"Sorry. Maybe you could find something from the warehouse where the crate was going? Surely there would have been other cargo."

"I could, except no one knows which one it is. It looks like the rest of the shipment was delivered direct to another part of town. A witness saw a wagon being driven away from the quay that night."

Just a wagon, of course, meant little. Plenty of wagons used the streets at night. Johanna remembered lying in bed in her room at the front of the house and hearing the sound of horse's hooves on the cobblestones. Wagons would come at night to pick up scraps, and sometimes even the peat man would still come after dark.

The memory was like a little stab of homesickness. Up here in the palace, she was so out of touch with those things. The best quality peat just appeared in the basket next to the hearth and she rarely even saw who put it there.

"Thank you for warning me about this," she said to Li Fai. "We will do our best to find out who the owner of this shipment is."

He made to get up, but hesitated.

"Is there anything else?"

"No, but . . ." He sighed. "My father asks that the guards punish those who are so keen to make us look like smugglers. Everyone in town seems to think that we've done some bad thing. When I walk in the street, mothers pull their children out of the way. People won't speak to me and scurry back into their houses."

"I don't think you're smugglers."

"No, but other people do." He took a deep breath and continued, "My father says that if you want his money, you should be more careful with who you let into your town." He looked at her when he said that, and there was an intense expression in his eyes.

"Just your father or do you speak for yourself as well?"

Did she see a flinch? "My father decides about our business. He does not like being accused of things we haven't done."

"But *you* know that this accusation of you is none of our doing?"

"I do." He flinched again and said, "But my father says it is made possible because your husband is a weak king."

Johanna could agree with that.

He took another deep breath and added, "He says you're a weak queen." Now he averted his eyes to the hands he held on his lap. His voice had lowered. "I'm sorry, that's what he says, whether I like it or not. He ordered me to say those things, so I have done right by him and said them."

Then he said in a lower voice, "My father does not understand. My father has no love for the art even if he employs sailors who have wind art for their advice on how to avoid storms and other hazards. He doesn't like the art and doesn't think that kings and emperors should get involved with it."

"Do you think I'm a weak queen?"

He said nothing for a while. His cheeks were red. Johanna's heart was thudding. She *was* a weak queen, dependent on the King's Council as she was. Because the nobles on the council didn't trust her, and because Roald wasn't going to make any decisions himself. And because they wouldn't let her make any decisions because she was a woman and they thought that she was stupid.

Li Fai said, "I prefer not to pass harsh judgement on people who treat us honourably."

In other words: he agreed that she was a weak queen.

"Tell me then, what should I do in your father's eyes? What does he say about me at the dinner table?"

"He says things that would not be wise to repeat." His cheeks grew red. "We are, in our culture, very open. We do not pretend things are better than they are. We do not say a thing to please someone, especially if that person is a friend."

The intense expression in his eyes made her squirm. "I am a weak queen. I would do so much more, but these men control every step I take, every decision that has to be made. I have to ask them to approve everything I want to do. Half the time, they don't. the other half, they dither until it is too late."

"My father says you should get rid of them."

Johanna snorted. "That's a lot easier said than done."

"He didn't say it would be easy either. He likes to work with strong rulers."

And she, clearly, didn't fit the bill.

A cold hand of panic clamped around her heart. Li Han might not even be interested in the investment in Saardam at all. He might simply hang around because King William and other royals were coming. Li Han might want to negotiate with them for better conditions of stay and hire of an office in Anglia or Lurezia.

Li Fai met her eyes and the look in them disturbed her. He reached out, briefly putting his hand on hers. He said, his voice low, "I want to stay. I think you're honourable. I think it is a great asset that you are not part of the royal families of the lowlands who are all related and intermarried, and who are all only interested in their own wealth. I would like to see you succeed."

His father, clearly, did not believe she could.

CHAPTER 2

JOHANNA WASN'T SURE how she made her way out of that room. She walked with Li Fai back to the hallway, with the back of her hand still tingling from his touch. She ached to reach for his hand and tell him that she wanted him to stay, too, that it didn't matter what his or her father said, or the King's Council, and that she didn't believe that he or his father smuggled guns or would do anything else that might cause harm to her position. But there were guards watching and while they could probably not hear the conversation, they would see everything.

Soon the rumours would be flying. *The queen has a lover.* And right now, in her situation, that would not look good.

So she felt very awkward walking next to him, not quite knowing what to do or say, and worrying that *not* saying anything would damage what little personal contact she had with him.

Li Fai's face showed no sign of such inner turmoil. He remained utterly aloof, like the prince she understood him to be.

The uncertainty ached inside.

They arrived in the cavernous foyer, where he bowed to her and left through the big doors that stood open to let in the fresh night air. Johanna stood at the top of the stairs watching him go down the stairs and cross the forecourt and walk out the gates.

She was a weak queen. Why, yes, she was, of course.

He *had* let it shine through that he didn't agree with his father's opinion of her, hadn't he?

That meant *he* didn't agree with his father, but he said the things his father had told him to say out of duty, hadn't he?

"Nice night, Your Majesty," a male voice commented.

Johanna startled. She had not noticed that the guard was so close. "Yes, it is indeed." Her heart thudded.

Where was the time that people didn't follow her around wherever she went? Why had she never appreciated her freedom?

She nodded to the guard, hoping that none of the guards noticed her inner turmoil, and then she cringed because caring what the guards thought of her was what made her weak. She should be ordering, not asking, and she should yell at them when they did something wrong.

With that one visit, Li Fai had brought her entire plan into doubt. She was weak. The kings and barons of the neighbouring countries would never listen to her.

She and Father had assumed, foolishly, that Li Han's support was a given. Father had met him before and they got along well. But clearly Li Han's patience was running out. So much of Johanna's proposal hinged on Li Han's presence with his iron ship, because if he went elsewhere, the reasons for neighbouring countries to care much about Saardam evaporated.

She had been too complacent, too lazy about proving her worth, because she had assumed that Li Han had reasons *not* to want to go to Lurezia. For one, King Benito was a cantankerous old man likely to introduce new taxes if foreigners annoyed him. He was unpredictable and had a reputation for hating any kind of change.

She had assumed that Li Han would *not* want to go to Anglia, because it was quite far away from the other lowland countries and the weather was dreadful for sailing a lot of the time.

But she might have been very, very wrong about those assumptions.

Johanna found Father at his desk in his room, meticulously drawing a building plan on a large piece of paper.

He looked up briefly when she came in, but continued his work, dipping his pen in the inkpot, drawing a couple of secure handstrokes. His work was slow but his hand still steady despite his age, and his work more ornate than hers because he had lots more patience.

"You should have asked Roald to help you," Johanna said. Roald was always drawing things.

Father snorted. "He would draw flowers in the corners." He kept working. "It's faster to do it myself. I've still got all that to copy."

He gestured at the pile on the corner of his desk, which contained outlines for proposed projects that the visitors could invest in. Once the visitors had all arrived, he and Master Deim would kick off the official part of the gathering with a trip around town to show the visitors the proposed sites for new buildings.

He was working so hard, and she hated disturbing him with unwelcome news.

"Li Fai was here," she began.

Father kept working, drawing precise pen strokes on the paper.

"He says that people have been using his brand to smuggle weapons."

Now he looked up sharply. Johanna told the story as she had heard it from Li Fai, leaving out his assessment of her style, telling of the noble taking delivery of the guns, but leaving out that she had seen the vision through the wood, because Father was still uneasy with the subject of magic.

He listened, his frown deepening. "I thought we had caught the young rascals who were falsifying Li Han's stamps."

Johanna sighed. "Yes, I thought so, too." She had also thought, foolishly, that Li Han was happy about the actions by the guards in punishment of those acts.

Father rubbed his chin. "And we don't know anything about who these smugglers are and where the stock is going?"

"Not yet. The guns are coming from somewhere inland. Burovia maybe." Although most of the Burovian trade came through Lurezia. "Or Montania."

"Florisheim," Father said, a dark expression on his face. "That's where a lot of illegal trade takes place. It's brought there by forest bandits, mountain bandits and other unsavoury scoundrels, to be distributed in the western regions. The Red Baron is not interested in controlling the illegal trade through his land because he makes money from it, and he probably uses some of those men as spies. If pressed, he argues that smugglers are on the Burovian side of the river anyway. King Leopold will argue that the bandits are not Burovian, so he can't do anything. That silly game has been going on for a long time."

"All the time with Li Han's stamp?"

"I doubt it. It's more likely that they used different disguises. But it's the same thing, even if Li Han's wares are a lot easier to recognise. Also the illegal importers might have latched onto the opportunity Li Han presented. A lot of people *want* Li Han to be guilty. They want to believe that he would do such a thing. Because he's foreign and strange to them, and they're afraid of the iron ship."

Johanna knew enough about that. Even after he'd been here for months, about half the King's Council were still opposed to his presence. Nobles, mostly, those belonging to the old guard of power, those who had controlled King Nicholaos before he became a supporter of the Church of the Triune.

Johanna shivered. Those men had connections much wider and more powerful than hers. "No one got a good description of the man on the deck of that ship taking delivery of those guns, except that he wore boots with silver buckles."

"That would apply to almost all nobles. Silver buckles are very popular."

"Were popular. They're a little bit passé now."

"What do I know about fashion?" Father spread his hands and both of them stared at the popping fire in the hearth. "Still, a good number of people would have shoes with silver buckles in their wardrobes. They would not wear their finest on a dark night on the quay."

That was true.

"This worries me, just before all our important guests are coming to town," Johanna said. "Any of them who arrive by ship will be mooring right there at the quay. Imagine people smuggling guns on the ship right next to King William's."

Johan Delacoeur loved to say that guns were not much good in battle—having poor aim and taking too long to reload—but were excellent for assassinations of important men.

She shuddered, thinking of what a terrible nightmare it

would be if something happened to King William or any of the other important guests.

Father nodded, his face serious.

Johanna said, "We need to find as many of these weapons as possible. Other shipments may have already gone out to wherever this was going, or still be in warehouses. We can't have entire shipments of guns lying about right next to where all the important people will be arriving. We need to know where they come from and what they're for."

"There is no way we can find out all those things. The guns will be for rebels, and they will be sold for money without much care about their purpose. There is a lot of talk about impending war, and people want to arm themselves. We don't have time to worry about any guns that have already reached their destination, only the ones that are still here. We will have to search all the warehouses. Johan Delacoeur can order that done."

"Does he have enough time for that?" Johan was always complaining that he didn't have enough men and that he had trouble finding good and trustworthy soldiers. During Alexandre's occupation of Saardam a lot of the younger men had left town to fight elsewhere or had been killed while defending their homes.

"We shouldn't need to check the entire city. Just the warehouses at the quay, and then they can close off the quay when the guests are arriving, and monitor their ships. We ask citizens for assistance. Many have no love for rogues or bandits and are afraid that someone like Alexandre will come back. They will report suspicious activity."

As Father spoke, Johanna knew that her ability could make a substantial difference to the chances of discovering caches of weapons in time. She must check the warehouses herself. Most of the buildings contained structural elements made of wood that could tell her stories of suspicious activity.

It was too late to do it today, but she would do that tomorrow at dusk, after church maybe. Add that to the incredible pile of things that needed to be done before the talks started, preferably before the guests arrived.

In a way, the thought of going into town alone, for the first time in months, excited her. She had been too complacent, too obedient, too tired to bother arguing against her advisers, too tired to even think for herself.

Father said that he was going to bed and Johanna also went to her private rooms. Her back ached, her feet were swollen and she was so tired that she could sleep for days. She'd be glad when this meeting was over and she could prepare herself for the birth of the child.

Roald lay on the couch in the sitting room, fully clothed and fast asleep, by the light of a sputtering lamp on the last of its oil. These past few weeks it had been warm enough to forego the fire, and Johanna quickly grabbed a candle to light it with the flame from the lamp before the room plunged into darkness.

During all this, Roald barely stirred. His face had acquired a healthy tan from all his work in the garden. His arms had become pleasantly muscled and his hair had bleached, which made the fact that his beard was red stand out more.

Johanna was happy that he liked gardening so much, but despaired at the prospect of having to make him appear at the meeting. He had not been to any King's Council meetings since the council was instated. When council member Theo Kloostermans met Roald in the hallways of the palace, he would ask some provocative political question, and then for the next week, the council would have to hear about the silly response, or lack of response, he got. Theo's agenda was pushing for the instatement of a regent, which happened to be Johan Delacoeur, who was of very distant royal blood through a king's illegitimate dalliances.

Theo didn't think Roald was fit to occupy the throne, and he wasn't.

Theo didn't think Johanna should be on the throne either, but that had to do with the lack of standing of her family. Theo was an old guard noble of a family closely associated with the Belaman Church.

On top of that, Theo was a belligerent, unpleasant character.

And Johanna was simply going to have to produce Roald at the very least during the opening dinner of the gathering. He would have to wear finery, and his crown, and would have to behave, give a short speech—which Johanna had written out but he'd so far refused to practice. All of this without laughing, squealing, banging his head on the table, rambling about gardening or about Rinius' theories—by the Triune, these were men of the Belaman Church which had hanged Rinius for being a heretic. And heaven forbid that any of the guests would bring their wives, because Roald *would* comment on the size of their "tits", loudly.

And clearly any failure on his part would be her fault. As it was, apparently, her fault that the king had a tanned skin like a peasant. Never mind that Roald was happy and she could handle all the rest, if only they let her.

She left him asleep on the couch and went back to the hallway, where she found Nellie in the linen room, putting away folded sheets.

She gasped when Johanna came up behind her. "Oh, mistress Johanna. I didn't see you. Look, I've got the bedding for the crib." She held up a small pile of white sheets with a pattern of flowers embroidered at the top.

Johanna tried to imagine a little baby in the bassinet that stood in the corner of the royal bedroom, but she could not. Yet this child was going to appear soon and that would bring even more trouble when the truth—that Roald wasn't the child's father—was immediately obvious.

She pushed away the unease that these days was never far under the surface. "I'm tired. I'm going to bed."

Nellie nodded. "I'll just finish putting these away and then I'll be there."

Johanna went to the bedroom and took off her dress. In only her underdress, she stood in front of the mirror, pulling the fabric tight over her swollen stomach. There was absolutely no hiding it in any way. She feared for the reaction of the important visitors, all of them men, when they saw her and whether they would still take her seriously. The King's Council was still getting over the fact that she didn't sit in her room with her feet up all day; but after destroying the old church relic, she had more or less demanded to be allowed to attend meetings, even if they said she should retire "in her condition".

There was a soft sound at the door and Nellie came in. She pulled back the stool at the dressing table. Johanna sat down. Nellie took the pins out of Johanna's hair, letting down the plait.

"How are you going with the preparations?" Johanna asked.

"We have the guest wing almost ready." King William's lodgings had been ready for a while, but with so many guests coming, the palace staff had worked hard to restore the previous guest wing to a state that visitors could use. It meant fixing up floors, walls and windows and, more recently, curtains, beds and furnishings.

"I'm sorry, Nellie, to cause you so much work."

"That's all right. It's kind of exciting anyway. Never in my wildest dreams would I have thought I'd ever see all these kings. Do you think they'll be bringing their wives?"

"Some will." Johanna thought of Baroness Viktoriya of Gelre and figured that was one wife they could do without. But she would never come. And King William wouldn't bring his wife. Apparently a lot of seamen considered it bad luck to have a woman on a ship.

"I've heard rumours that King Benito will bring his wife," Nellie said.

"Would that be his fourth or fifth?"

Nellie sniffed. "Mistress Johanna, that is an unkind remark."

"Well, apparently he divorced all of them because he still has no heir. One would think that he was the problem."

"Oh, mistress Johanna!" But the rebuke came with a laugh. Nellie had changed recently, become less nervous and happier. Maybe the thought that she would look after the baby princess made her happy. For as long as the princess was little at least, Nellie would have a doll to dress up in pretty clothes. But if omens were anything to go by, the little princess would need her magic sooner rather than later, and Johanna would make sure that she learned how to use it for good, and how to fight the evil coming from the man who was probably her father.

Johanna shivered. She always felt the chill of magic coursing through her when she thought about Kylian. It still upset her that she could not remember what had happened at the farmhouse of the Guentherite order. Some part of her still hoped that the child was Roald's and that all her worries would be for nothing.

Nellie finished combing her hair and retrieved an earthenware jar with a wooden stopper from the drawer. "Do you want me to do this now?"

"Yes, please." Johanna sat on the bed, and Nellie rubbed ointment into the skin of her legs and stomach. It was a concoction given to her by Helena to help with the itchiness of the stretched skin on Johanna's belly. It was an affliction common for women in her situation, Helena had said. The ointment helped a little, but it had a pungent smell.

"You're getting to be so big," Nellie said. "If I didn't know any better I would think you were about to burst."

Johanna felt like that. She'd been having trouble sleeping, and walking any distance was getting difficult. And sometimes when the child wriggled it gave her a painful kick in the ribs. But Helena said the end of August, and Helena knew about these things.

"To be honest, I wouldn't mind if it ended sooner." Johanna shuddered at the thought of what would happen when the child came. Sometimes when she lay awake at night she could still hear Greetje's screams.

Of course Greetje had gone to her husband a long time ago, and looked happy with her fair-haired little boy. She had long since forgotten the ordeal.

"One more week," Johanna said with a sense of determination. "Then I'm going to ask Helena if she has something to make the child come."

She'd heard women talk about a special tea they drank, and some kind of seed that women would shove up their—well, where the child came out—and that the poisons leaked from the coating would bring on the pains.

Nellie rubbed ointment into the firm skin with a gentle movement. Where this used to be relaxing, Nellie's touch now made Johanna's stomach cramp up. Johanna winced and pushed Nellie's hands away.

"But I thought this made you feel better?"

"Not anymore."

In all reality, nothing made much of a difference in her level of comfort anymore. She was tired, bloated and everything she did every day hurt: walking, sitting, lying down, eating too much, eating too little, even pissing and not to mention that pooping had become a major source of anxiety and agony.

By the time Johanna changed into her nightgown, Roald had woken up and shuffled into the bedroom, carrying a book.

Nellie left, after having lit the candles on the bedside table.

Roald climbed into bed and opened his book.

By the Triune, he needed a haircut. His beard was getting unruly, too.

"Maybe you need to see a barber before the guests arrive," she said.

He pulled a face.

"The visitors start arriving tomorrow," Johanna continued. "I would like it if you didn't look like a bandit."

He didn't react. He was leafing through the illustrations of plants. Johanna knew this was not the case, but sometimes she felt like he was ignoring her on purpose.

She tried again. "I will ask the barber to see you tomorrow."

"I have carrots to be harvested."

"Yes, and they're very nice. Did you look at that speech I wrote for you?"

"You can give it."

"No, Roald, I can't." She leaned closer to him. "There are some things I can't do, because people don't accept it when I do them." There were many such things, actually. "You're the king."

"Yes. That means I get to do exactly what I want."

"It doesn't *quite* work like that."

"Oh yes, it does. The garden was my idea. It's very nice and we're giving lots of food to the poor people."

And that was true, too. They had even started giving away young hens to people with families. "I know what we're doing is good, but I still need you to come. I still need you to visit the barber. I still need you to make that speech. It's short. I would like you to come to at least one of the meetings to make it clear that I have your blessing."

No reaction. He looked at his book.

Johanna put her hand over the page. "Roald, listen." She crouched so that he was forced to look her in the eyes. "This meeting is very important to Saardam. King William is going to arrive. King Leopold will be there, and Baron Uti, and King Benito. We don't want to give them the wrong impression."

"Everyone of those people already knows that I'm an idiot."

"But you can prove that you're not. Because you aren't."

"I'm the idiot king! I don't need to learn the speech. I know it already. Welcome esteemed guests. We welcome to our table the King of Gluttony, the baron and his wife with giant evil tits." And he started laughing.

"Roald! You can't talk about our guests like that."

"I'm right, though. And everyone agrees, but they're all too scared to say so."

"You can't say that. We want to get them to invest their money in our city. We don't want to anger them."

He fixed her with that eerily innocent expression of his. "They talk about me when I'm not listening. They don't like me. I don't like them. I don't want to pretend-like them."

And that was as much as she got out of him. Father had given her the task to prepare Roald for the meeting, but so far that project had been an utter failure. She didn't want him at the dinner because it would be a disaster. Yet he had to be there, at least for the opening, at least to show the guests that he cared.

She remembered Roald giving a speech at his welcome ball, and dancing with girls. She remembered thinking that he was really odd, but now that she knew more, she realised what an incredible achievement it was for him to even have come that far.

How had Queen Cygna managed to get him to cooperate?

CHAPTER 3

BUT JOHANNA couldn't ask anyone how to get Roald to do his kingly duties. None of the people who had prepared him back when he gave a speech at the ball were still alive. She shuddered to think how much work that would have taken, and threats, and how petrified he would have been.

She realised that if she had wanted Roald to be obedient, she should have treated him as one treated a naughty child from the moment they got married. Some of the nobles made whispers in that general direction, that she should be "firm with him", and give him no option but to cooperate. But Roald was not a child, and she didn't like the idea of treating him like one.

She paid the price for that way of thinking now.

After breakfast the next morning, she went into the garden with him to try and talk to him while he worked.

He told her several times that he didn't want to go, but mostly just pottered about the garden beds and talked about his plants. He chased ducks back into their pen, fed the chickens and harvested beans with childish enthusiasm.

Anyone would say that he was ignoring her on purpose, but Johanna knew that wasn't true. It was just that when he got into a mindset, he was incapable of listening to anything else.

Even arguments that would work with children had no effect on him. He was not interested in food. He could not be bribed with trips. He cared little about material things and even less about pleasing people he liked. In fact, she doubted that he cared as much about people, including her, as he cared about the garden or the horses. And things that did interest him, like books or study, weren't hers to promise. In fact, the less said about his obsession with Rinius, the better.

And as she sat there on the bench to take the weight off her sore feet, sipping tea brought by a maid and watching Roald pull weeds out of the carrot beds, she knew that *she* didn't want to force him. He had his plants and his ducks and chickens. He didn't know how to communicate with people and the idea of trying to force him made her ill.

But he *had* to be present at least at the dinner. She'd already had an argument with Father about that. And everyone considered Roald her responsibility, except he was a grown man, and the king to boot, and the one thing he understood about his position was that he could do exactly as he pleased.

As usual, her efforts to talk to him pretty much ended in nothing. He didn't listen, he argued about the smallest bits of trivia and latched onto details that didn't matter.

It got quite warm in the garden, and Johanna went back inside, tired, frustrated and despairing of what to do.

The guests would be here soon. Roald hated most of them and would not hesitate telling them so. And yes, when she was a child, she had also despaired of Father's complaining at the dinner table that he had to deal with so-and-so and then later watched him be perfectly nice to this person. It was odd, when you thought about it.

It was called *growing up*. Learning to lie with a straight face, for the sake of harmony, business or some other grown-up cause.

Roald was very much still a little child.

She sat at her desk, but grew too uncomfortable with her belly pressing against the edge of the table and her upper back sore from trying to bend over so that she could still see what she was writing. She was too tired to concentrate.

Maybe Li Han was right. Maybe she was as weak and inadequate as some in the King's Council said she was. Maybe it was more important that Roald be kept as a puppet, performing his puppetlike duties, than that he be happy.

Maybe she'd done everything wrong for the past year and maybe all her plans were about to unravel.

The desktop blurred before her eyes. She was so tired, so sore, so much still needed to be done and she was too tired to do it.

So instead of working, she lay down on the couch and promptly fell asleep. But not even her naps were pleasant anymore. She dreamed that she was sitting in the Red Room talking to all these important guests and that Roald came in with a gun. He started shooting people, and strange enough everyone stayed in heir seats. When she asked why, an over-dressed noble told her that it was a payback for all the times they had laughed at Roald. Then there was a bang and his brains flew everywhere.

Johanna sat up, sweating.

The bang had been caused by Father entering the room. "Johanna?"

Johanna struggled to sit.

"Are you all right?" There was concern on his face.

"Yes, just . . . I fell asleep. I'm so tired."

"You shouldn't try to do everything. We have the situation

under control. King Leopold and his entourage have just arrived. They're being taken to their quarters now."

King Leopold and his party would be staying in the beautiful Mayor's house where repairs had just been completed after minor fire damage and more substantial damage from wild parties held by Alexandre's cronies. Joris Decamp himself was still living in his old house so that the restored house could be used as guesthouse for the visiting royals, because even with hasty restorations, the palace did not have enough suitable rooms for that many royal guests.

Father went on, "Johan went to meet King Leopold and his party. He and the king served together in the Border Forest war."

That had been long before Johanna was born, in southern Burovia. Men and their war connections could be a mystifying thing, but she was glad that someone else handled King Leopold. No doubt he and whoever else arrived before tomorrow night would be at dinner in the palace on the night before the meetings started.

In the afternoon, she managed to get Roald to sit still for long enough for the barber to trim his hair and beard.

Next, Helena came to see her, and completed her examinations with a frown that did not leave her face. Not happy, clearly. To Johanna's complaint about finding it hard to do her business, she suggested eating prunes.

"They're in season, and they will make it soft—very soft if you eat a lot of them. It's very common with women in your condition to have this trouble. The child is sitting very low."

That was not a good thing, apparently. To Johanna's questions about tea or seeds to bring on the birth, Helena made a non-committal reply that she would bring some.

Johanna heard *if you need it* in her words and a wave of panic came over her. "Is the child going to come early?"

"There is a good chance."

"But that's impossible with all these guests here."

Helena chuckled and shook her head. "When a child is ready, it's ready. It waits for no kings or priests or weather."

Johanna met her eyes, a feeling of horror creeping over her. Helena's message added to the constant messages her body was giving her: you don't have as long as you planned. The child decided when it came.

By the Triune.

And yes, she had known that.

All her fatigue was gone in one hit. As soon as Helena left, she went to her office and completed all the work that had seemed impossible to do this morning. Then she went to the bedroom. She dragged the cabinet that held the bedpan and water pitcher to the side so that Helena would be able to put the birthing chair in front of the window. She climbed up the little stool and retrieved some pillows from the top shelf of the wardrobe. She put them against the footrest of the bed so that they were ready.

She took a tiny little singlet and a couple of wrapping cloths from the wardrobe and put those on top of the cabinet next to the bassinet. Nellie had already fixed the bedding. Johanna pushed back the veil so that the child could go straight in.

Then she noticed that where the cabinet had stood in front of the window, the floor was dusty, and she went to the corridor to find a broom.

She swept the rest of the room, too, because there was some dust under the bed.

Father came to have a look what she was doing, and she informed him, "Just making sure everything is ready."

He raised his eyebrows, but left her alone.

After the evening meal, which was the last one they took in relative quiet, Johanna dressed to go out.

She had one night to go out to the warehouses to check

on the gun smuggling business. She owed it to Li Fai to try to find out who was taking delivery of those guns.

She asked Anton of the guard to get her a coach.

"I need to get an account book from the office," she told Father when he was curious about it.

"Why not ask one of the boys to get it for you?"

"I just want to go out, see something else, before . . ." She spread her hands and left the matter of whether she meant before the meeting or before the child was born up to him to decide. Both probably. And, also, she fervently hoped that she wasn't giving the impression that she was going to visit Li Fai, because Father was the sort of person who saw through everything. If people were going to gossip about the two of them in that way, she wanted their gossip to be true.

Sitting on the bench in the coach, watching the city streets go by through the little window, she let her imagination run rampant. In the vision she had seen when he first gave her the magical box that she carried in her purse, they had sat in the meadow on the outskirts of the city, and he had kissed her. When she had asked about it, he'd said the box showed *possible* futures, not certain or probable futures. But she could not help wondering why it had showed her that.

Because you wanted it? a little voice inside her said, and by the Triune, she did. Meeting him again after trying to avoid him for two months had made that clear to her. She'd hoped that his absence from her life would make her forget what she felt when she saw him, but if anything she had gone from wanting to feel his mouth on hers to aching to take him inside her, and having him please her in a way that Roald had done only twice, and then by accident.

Lately he had been completely disinterested.

What if she casually dropped in at the iron ship and asked Li Fai a lame question? She could ask him to come with her to inspect the warehouses *just for her safety*. They would be in the dark by themselves, which would give him plenty of opportunities to . . .

Would he do what she so desperately wanted?

Or did she misinterpret his smiles and gentle touches, and would meeting him again leave her heartbroken?

No, she couldn't afford to let herself be distracted. She'd go and see him later. Right now, she desperately needed to check the warehouses for activities that might endanger the influential guests.

But if there was one thing she feared resulting from this meeting of kings and barons and other important people, it was that Li Han would decide to go elsewhere and take his son with him.

Then you've just got to show him why he should stay, that little voice said inside her head told her. Normally her little voices sounded like Master Deim, but she couldn't imagine that he would give her this advice. Father wouldn't, either. Make no mistake, they both would like Li Han to stay, but it was about the iron ships, not about his son's sharp eyes and his muscled shoulders, and the way he looked at her when she spoke about magic.

The coach came to a halt at the quay in front of Father's office. Anton jumped off the driver's seat to open the door and helped Johanna out. Over the past month or so, the little ladder had become so awkward that he almost supported her entire weight.

"Are you sure you don't want me to come?" he asked.

"Just watch from here," Johanna said. "You can casually walk along the quay, but don't follow too closely. I don't want to draw attention to myself."

Judging by the look on his face, he didn't like it, but didn't protest.

Johanna went up the few steps to the front door to Father's office. When she opened it, the familiar smell of spices and tobacco wafted out. It was also mixed with a faint tang of must. These days Father didn't use the office very much anymore.

On a coat stand in the hallway hung a heavy cloak that Father would use to go out onto the boats when it rained. Johanna put it on over her regular clothes. It didn't shut at the front, because her belly was too big, but she pulled the sides as close together as they would go. The hood went over her hair so that it would shade her face. She then snuck out the back entrance that once would have provided entry for servants and minor workers.

It came out into a narrow alley where the looming walls on both sides took away almost all of the light still remaining of the day. Even after almost a full year since the invasion by Alexandre and his bandits, the faint tang of burnt wood still hung in corners where not many people came. The houses behind the office had been damaged, and half-burned beams had been removed from the roofs and dumped in the alley.

Johanna followed the narrow walkway to where it opened out into the street that ran back to the waterfront. A few people came the other way in the street, but it was dark, her hood hid her face, and Saardam was big enough that not everyone immediately knew everyone else by the way they walked.

It was a good feeling to be free again and not recognised. Although it would be even nicer without that big belly.

She glanced over her shoulder at the coach that still stood in front of the office, with Anton standing next to it. No doubt he had seen her, because he idly wandered along the quayside in her direction. Johanna turned away from him, making her way along the quayside to the warehouses. But walking was not as easy as it had once been. Her legs hurt and, with each step, the child bumped into her bladder. That caused the constant sensation that she needed to pee, which she had learned to ignore as much as she could, but by the Triune, it made walking an excruciating agony, especially for any distance. The far side of the quay, normally a short stroll away, became an almost unreachable target.

Coming here might not have been her best idea ever.

But Johanna gritted her teeth and slowly made her way down, stopping frequently to catch her breath or let her poor legs recover, putting her hand or this or that wooden pole or fence or window frame.

She saw images of ships arriving—yes, King Leopold was definitely here. He had arrived in a sleek and ornate river sloop that lay moored at the quay, guarded by two men with lots of shiny metal decorations on their uniforms. The ship's large cabin made it suitable for the transport of passengers only. It had a harness for no less than ten sea cows. She could see King Leopold coming down the gangplank. He was a short rotund man who had so little hair that he wore horse-hair wigs, mostly black, because he was known to say that white horsehair made him look old.

The quayside immediately in front of Father's office was still empty. This space was reserved for King William's ship, which would be an ocean-faring vessel with a deep keel that needed the deepest part of the harbour.

Anton followed her at a distance, but she didn't want to make it too clear what she was doing. After having been to Master Willems' house when she and Li Fai dealt with the old church relic, Anton would know about magic, but he had never said anything about what had happened in that house.

Johanna finally arrived at the eastern end of the harbour and stopped for another rest. The buildings here sheltered the quayside and adjacent water from the breeze. The moonlight reflected in the oily surface of the still water, rippling only when something moved underneath.

Fish, she hoped.

This was the spot where Auguste LaFontaine had drowned. It was close to the spot where she and Nellie had fished Roald out of the water on the night that the city was ablaze and all seemed lost.

It was also close to the spot where, a month ago, ships with teams of sea cows and horses had finally removed the wreckage of the *Lady Davida*, burned and too damaged to be salvaged. The deck hand Adrian's body had not yet been found.

There was so much death here.

CHAPTER 4

AFTER A SHORT REST, Johanna kept going.

A string of warehouses along the eastern quay jutted out into the wide expanse of the river. Father's sea cow barn and the *Lady Sara* were right at the very end, but in order to get to them, you needed to walk past all the warehouses. The ships that had been moved from the main quay to make space for the dignitaries lay double-moored along this side. Li Han's ship was a familiar shadow against the moonlit water: solid and stubby, with a single fat chimney protruding from the deck. A storm light hung at the top deck, where there was just enough of a breeze to make the flame flap. Its light produced a pool of yellowish glow that lit the side of the cabin. Someone's washing hung there, and Johanna could also see a part of the cage that she knew contained fat grey and white ducks.

She stared at it, willing Li Fai to come out of the cabin and talk to her. But all remained quiet and she knew it was better that way

She went into the first warehouse on her right. It used to belong to a fabric merchant but now it was being used for the storage of food. As soon as she opened the door, little squeaks in the darkness betrayed the scurrying of mice. She walked along an aisle between two bays of shelves, but away from the door it soon became so dark that it was impossible to see. She touched the wood of the shelving, but saw nothing that indicated a need for further investigation. Just quay workers unloading and loading freight. Chatting to each other. The warehouse manager ordering them around. Where to go, what to bring, where to put it.

She continued to the next warehouse, which contained furniture and carpets. The wood here told stories of couches being moved around. The owner's wife had a fair bit to say in the business. She ran the warehouse and did the accounts while the husband talked to customers. Johanna recognised the couple and was glad that they had survived.

The next warehouse was the timber shed where Nellie had found the chips that told the story of Li Han's stamp being falsified. The owner had been questioned and a web of smuggling unmasked. The owner had then sold the business to an honest man. The wood chips and shavings on the ground and the planks in shelves against the walls told stories of young men working hard.

Johanna sank to her knees and dug in the woodchips, but none of the stories she found there were particularly interesting or relevant.

The next warehouse was a shipyard. The back door of the shed was open, and the reflection from the moonlit river out that way silhouetted the skeletons of boats that stood in the dry docks in the process of being built. The wooden hulls of the boats told stories of men sweating over fires to melt the tar to seal the gaps between the planks in the hull. It fascinated her to see how this was done, but told her nothing about gun smuggling.

Half the shed was also over the water. The sea cows down there snorted and chewed noisily.

It was really dark here, and Johanna didn't want to risk falling in the water, so she made her way back to the entrance.

Well, that was a waste of time. Clearly the weapons weren't being stored in the harbour, as Li Fai had suggested.

She looked again at Li Han's ship. A little voice in her mind kept telling her to come up with excuses to go up that steep gangplank, where she'd been only once before, and where the ducks would start quacking, and where Li Fai would come from the cabin to check out the racket.

She wanted to go up there so badly, but she couldn't. Li Han was one of the guests at the upcoming meeting, by the Triune. He was not a guard to be taken into confidence about the risks posed to visitors by smuggled guns. He was one of the visitors who needed to be protected against the man with the silver-buckled shoes whose identity she was no closer to discovering.

But hey, something was now going on across the harbour.

Between the tall bow of Li Han's ship and the much lower deck of the *Lady Sara*, she noticed movement of people with lights on the deck of a ship on the other side of the harbour, a river sloop that lay moored on the harbour side hiding behind King Leopold's ship.

The vessel was sleek and dark, with a low cabin that had numerous windows with closed curtains. Wasn't that the ship that had brought Roald back before the ball that started all this misery? The Burovian ship that belonged to the Guentherite brotherhood?

Yes, she was almost sure it was.

That could mean only one thing: *Kylian* was here. The ship's position, moored alongside the Burovian king's ship, betrayed the relationship between Baron Uti, his cousin King

Leopold and the Guentherite order of the Belaman Church that practiced necromancy and magic.

She should have known there was a good chance that Kylian would turn up with his father, but it was especially galling that he dared walk into *her* city.

She peered into the darkness, but was too far away to recognise any of the people on the deck. She didn't *think* Kylian was one of them, but he would be there.

A chill came over her despite the warm weather. The cold went deep inside her belly, where the child squirmed and kicked. There was magic in the air, and even if she couldn't feel it, the child could. She clamped her arms around herself.

She had best go back to Anton. Kylian would feel it if she used her magic, and she did *not* want to encounter him in the dark alone.

But there was a soft noise closer to where she stood. Her first thought was *a rat*, but the sound came from her right, somewhere in the water.

Johanna took a few steps so that she could see around the bow of Li Han's ship and peered into the darkness.

Something *glowed* underneath the surface of the water.

By the Triune, that looked like . . .

She had seen things like this before . . . in Florisheim, where ghosts emerged from the water and wandered over the surface . . . because at the Guentherite brotherhood's farm, a deep hole dug in the ground to find black rock had disturbed the spirits of the dead. And because Kylian was practicing his necromancy, bringing ghosts back to their bodies.

Johanna watched, her heart thudding.

The underwater glow made a little dome in the water's surface, and then broke the surface. The silvery, glowing blob that came out took a while to acquire a shape. First it grew a bud at the top, and then two smaller buds on each side of the bigger one. Those two grew long and thin, waving at the sky.

The top bud grew into a head with long flowing hair. The rest of the shape elongated and became a body in a thin, elfinlike dress.

The ghost of Princess Celine had returned to Saardam.

She walked over the water to the Guentherite brotherhood's ship. The men on the deck had gone below. She put her hands on the bow, looking up at the railing. When no one came, she threw her head back and wailed. It was a sound lighter than the wind, colder than ice, sharper than glass. It chilled Johanna deep inside.

A man climbed to the deck and looked over the railing. She reached out for him with both hands, but he slapped her aside. She fell to her knees, wailing, sitting on the water's surface as if it was solid.

The man threw an object at her. She flew up and threw the object back at him.

His laughter echoed over the water. Magic erupted from his hand, engulfing her. She sank back under the water.

By the Triune. Was that Kylian?

He straightened and looked over the water as if he sensed her.

A chill went through Johanna. Her stomach cramped up. By the Triune, she suddenly needed to pee so badly that it hurt.

The door to Father's sea cow barn was directly behind her. There would be a bucket in there to do her business.

Johanna stumbled to the door, pain lancing through her stomach with each step. The child squirmed inside her, wedging some body part under her ribs. She winced. That hurt, little one.

Johanna pulled the door open—

And she stopped.

A small fire burned on the paved floor in the loading area. Two figures in dark robes crouched by the fire, both small and thin and dressed in rags. Oh by the Triune, why did Father's barn always attract beggars?

She stammered, "I'm sorry. I thought . . ." But she didn't know what she thought or what she could say to a couple of urchins. She didn't look like a fellow beggar. She didn't even look like a fishwife. She hoped they weren't familiar enough with the royal family to know who she was. Come to think of it, she should probably get out of here and let Anton deal with it.

But then one of the two beggars lowered the hood of his tattered old cloak, and it was not a *him* but a *her*.

Johanna recognised the pale, wide-eyed face. She gasped. "Loesie!"

By the Triune, she had changed so much. She looked taller, her eyes more alert, and her expression more vicious. Johanna wanted to hug her, but something stopped her. Loesie looked . . . formidable, and suddenly so much older. Her hair had always been dark, but now it had gone even darker, flecked through with a few white hairs at the temples.

The person with her was also a woman. She looked younger than Loesie, had flaxen blond hair like Nellie and a round face with freckles.

She would have been pretty if it weren't for her eyes. Mist whirled within the milky white irises.

The air grew cold. A chilling breeze ruffled her hair. Johanna didn't have the ability to feel magic in the air, but she was certain that if she could, she would be staggering back from the magic force that radiated from this woman. The child inside her kicked her hard in the ribs.

This had to be Kylian's magic, there was no doubt about it.

Loesie said, "Yes, we came back. We saw on the wind that a lot of fuss be happening. We figured this be where the action is."

"Did you see Kylian? He's on a boat on the other side of the harbour." She put her hand on the curve of her stomach to calm herself down.

"Why do you think we's hiding in here? It's warm enough to sleep outside and if we didn' have to, we sure wouldn' be sleeping in s stinky shed with slobbering and farting animals."

To illustrate Loesie's words, one of the sea cows swam past, leaving a trail of bubbles, while munching noisily on a chunk of cabbage.

"You are certainly welcome back," Johanna said.

Despite the magic in the other woman's eyes, there was something reassuring and familiar about Loesie's words. *This* was her old Loesie. Johanna had never been happy with the Loesie who, after having been cured of her possession by Duke Lothar, lost her country accent. "You and your friend can stay here. It's not like Father is using the barn a lot these days."

"This here be Annette. She were on my granma's farm. She were dead but she came back to life. She be demon-touched so don' get too close to her."

"Thanks for warning me." Johanna had no such intention. Each time she looked at the young woman, she felt a chill.

Loesie said, "And look at you. The babe is close, I can feel it."

Johanna responded automatically, "Another month."

"Hmmm." She clearly didn't believe that.

"What are you doing here?" Johanna asked, pushing away unease. She wanted the child to stay put until after the meeting. "You're not selling cheese?"

"We's sold some. The farm still needs money to pay for clothes and all that."

"Did any other people of your family survive? I thought they were all gone."

"Only the demon-touched survived. We be a whole farm

of bewitched women and children, working the fields through magic. But we still need eatin', so that's why we be selling the cheese. That and we be following the ghosts that have floated down the river."

"Did you notice them when they came past the farm?"

"No. They'd be coming from Gelre. The necromancer brought them. He's been travelling the river for years. He made ghosts everywhere. They's all in the water."

"That long? You never said anything about it?"

"I were bewitched. Even when we came back here, I were not myself. The Duke took part of it away, and then I washed the rest off in the river. Then I helped the girls."

"Girls?"

"Them's the ones he needed. The necromancer journeyed all along the river up and down and up and down, killing and raping. He killed those he could not rape. And he killed the rest after he raped them. Like poor Annette here, they's stuck in between life and death. Except he can't easily kill the ones with magic, and he can't kill the ones who's become with child after he's raped them so those ones came to the farm, often with bleeding wounds from where he's tried to kill them."

By the Triune. Johanna felt sick. "How many of you?"

"We's a group of twenty-one. Other farms, I don't know. The Duke knows how many. There's other places where they hide besides our farm."

Johanna thought of the work farm at the Guentherite brotherhood. "How many of those women are Kylian's minions doing his bidding?"

"We's not minions. He might wish we were. The farm be a safe place where the women can hide from him. We had six babes born just this month. If the mother's been badly touched by him, she dies, and we have an extra mouth to feed a long time before we have a pair of hands to work on the farm and a magician to teach. They's more worry for us."

"You teach magic now?"

"No, I'm no teacher. The teacher be the duke. He comes to visit. We keep the children alive and busy."

"Is the duke here?"

"Not yet, but he be coming, bringing some other girls. The necromancer is up to something."

Didn't Johanna know about that.

But when Johanna asked, Loesie didn't know what Duke Lothar planned or when he would arrive. She didn't know what sort of magic, locations, relics or substances he would be using.

That was the thing that frustrated her most about people with magic: they did not plan, and they did not let others know what they were doing. Or maybe the duke had announced his plans, and Loesie had not paid attention. Loesie was the worst person to ask about these types of things.

Johanna said, "I don't know how often I can come to see you here. We have all the important guests arriving, and I'd be lying if I said I had any time to come and see you, because I don't. This is the last night before they all start coming into town."

"Don't be worried," Loesie said. "You look after the important people. They's all non-magical anyway. They only need to be kept busy, and they won't even see that there's something going on. They think they's important, but they's all so dumb. You look after them. We'll look after the magic."

Johanna wasn't sure it was so simple. For one, Kylian would come for *her* and the child; but for the time being, she could do nothing else.

CHAPTER 5

JOHANNA RETURNED in the coach to that exact same spot on the quay the next morning for a completely different reason. The harbourmaster had sent word to the palace of King William's arrival, and this important guest needed special attention. So she had dressed in a formal but not too flamboyant dress, asked Nellie to do her hair, and clambered into the coach. Father sat on the bench opposite her, wearing the formal Carmine family coat that Mistress Dina had made for him. The weather was rather too warm for it, and beads of sweat pearled on his forehead.

Johanna wasn't feeling the best after her foray the previous night. Her legs were tired, her feet so swollen that they almost wouldn't fit into her shoes, and the chill of magic that had stabbed through her belly had never completely subsided. She *knew* that the child had magic, and that almost certainly meant that it was Kylian's, as she feared—and as, according to Loesie, seemed to have happened to a lot of other girls. What was Kylian's game?

She sat in the coach entertaining dark thoughts while summer turned out one of the most beautiful days this year.

The sky was brilliant blue and the painted houses made a pretty picture that belied the city's damaged state.

There were a lot of people on the quay, most of them watching from the deck of ships or from the steps or upstairs windows to offices. The mooring in front of Father's office, which had been vacant last night, was now taken up by an impressively large ship.

Because they were both seafaring nations competing to discover new lands, Saarland and Anglia had been at war several times. The countries were currently in a period of stalemate in which both did their best to ignore each other. Not openly hostile, not friendly either. It had been a long time since an Anglian ship was sighted in the harbour. In fact, Johanna could only remember one time, when she was very little. That had been a merchant ship nowhere near as impressive as the king's flagship.

The three-master towered over Saardam's fleet of river sloops and over the buildings that lined the quay, and most of those were over two floors high.

The ship's masthead, the Anglian long-horned bull bowing its head, ready to attack, loomed over the stern of King Leopold's otherwise impressive river sloop. The ship's name was *Targon*, after the Anglian capital, painted in silver letters on the bow. The hull was dark, of sleeker design than the Saarlander seafaring ships. It was said that she could outrun most of the pirate ships that inhabited the southern Lamorian Ocean. Most of the many sails hung loose and deck hands were in the masts and webbing to stow them. A line of uniformed soldiers stood on the poop deck overlooking the harbour with stern faces and lances by their sides.

The gangplank was down, and two rows of armed soldiers

stood guard on either side. They wore the typical red jackets of the Anglian guard, complete with their distinctive caps with the dangling fox's tail.

Their trumpets glittered, the sails flapped, the paintwork on the ship's deck shone with bright colours, and brilliant gold and glittering silver.

Father stared at the ship through the little window in the coach's door, like a young boy in a lolly shop.

Compared to the ship, her coach was rather plain, as she had thought appropriate for the fact that most of Saardam still suffered deprivation and hardship. Anton and his colleague on the driver's seat were well-clad and looked dapper, but they weren't a smidgen on these Anglian guards.

The difference was quite unsettling and made Johanna think that she might have made a mistake. Pomp and ceremony intimidated people. It made people believe that a kingdom, a family, an estate, was the best and richest ever. When people were impressed, they were more likely to accept what a person said. She really *should* get more flamboyant dresses, pretty up the coach and furnish the palace with the most extravagant decorations, but it didn't seem fair to her when many people in Saardam barely had roofs over their heads.

Fair: another word that *real* kings and queens never cared about.

Would she ever get over the feeling that one day, someone would come and say "She's only a commoner!" and would put her right where she belonged?

The bugles sounded. The coach stopped. Anton jumped off the driver's seat, walked past the side and opened the door, letting in bright sunlight. Johanna rose, a little awkwardly in that dress.

The herald shouted, "Hail Queen Johanna of Saarland!" People cheered.

He shouted again, "Hail King William of Anglia."

People cheered again.

Johanna used Anton's hand to climb down from the coach and waited until Father was down as well. The Saarlander guard had cleared a path from the coach to the ship. Walking between those rows of people on Father's arm, Johanna felt very small. The weight of a lot of expectations rested on her shoulders.

She and Father waited at the bottom of the gangplank while the visiting party came down in slow steps, a gaggle of ornate hats, rich velvet jackets, shirts with lots of frills, and high-heeled boots. Even though Johanna had never met King William, there was little doubt about which of them was the king.

He was a tall man without being gangly. He had curly ginger-blond hair which he wore in a loose ponytail at the back of his head, a red face and startling blue eyes.

The other companions were all men, and two were guards in uniform. Another one was a scribe of some sort, carrying a leather-bound book and the last one . . . he was of fine build and walked behind the king as a servant, but he wasn't dressed like one. He had grey eyes and soft flaxen hair which hung loose over his shoulders. He wore a blue hat with a big feather, light blue trousers and a shirt with an excessive display of frills. He carried a watch or compass of some sort on a gold chain, and had lots of rings on his fingers. He was far too old to be the king's son, and too different in build to be a brother.

King William stepped off the gangplank onto the quay. He looked around with his thumbs hooked in his belt, and said, "Say, where is the king of this godforsaken place?"

Johanna gritted her teeth. "We welcome you to our city, Your Majesty. I am sure nothing here is new to you. I hope your travels have been favourable. I am Queen Johanna—"

"The lass who invited me?"

Several people took in sharp breaths.

Johanna straightened her back. She had been warned about him. "I invited you, yes. And thank you for coming. This here is my advisor, Dirk Brouwer." She gestured at Father.

King Williams let out a loud laugh that echoed over the water and no doubt could be heard by everyone at the quay. "A merchant? A merchant is the king's chief adviser?"

He was really starting to annoy her. She corrected, "The queen's advisor, and yes, a merchant. We want to become the lowland city where everyone comes to trade, sell and buy. *We* ask the experts."

Another round of gasps. This remark referred to one of the more recent sea battles between the two countries, involving King William's father, that Saardam had won because Anglia had taken strategic advice from a noble who had no interest or knowledge in the matter of sea battles.

But King William let out another very loud burst of laughter. "Ha, ha, ha, you have spunk in you. I like that. You'll get along fine with my court advisor. This is Earl Maximilian Clarendon de Blasisse."

The little man in the light blue outfit bowed. "It is an honour to finally meet you, milady." Even his voice was whiny and foppish.

Johanna met Father's eyes over the earl's head. What a strange character. "Do accompany us to the palace where your accommodation is ready. We will send our servants to collect your necessities."

Johanna preceded him to the coach, again traversing the path in between walls of curious onlookers.

Her coach had room for six, but King William was so tall that he took up two seats—after having almost banged his head on the doorframe. Johanna let the king and his companion have the forward-facing seats while she and Father took the rearward-facing ones. The king sat spread out in the middle seat, pushing the little foppish Earl against the side of the coach. The king's legs were so long that Johanna and Father each had to sit to the side as well, and still his left leg kept brushing her dress, which was distracting. He looked pointedly at her belly, but said nothing about it, which at least was a welcome change from King Leopold, whom she had barely seen but had already managed to inform her, "Your husband should be ashamed that you have to work in this state."

The coach jumped into motion and the harbour slid from view.

No one spoke inside the cabin.

Johanna felt intensely uncomfortable facing this tall, red-bearded, blue-eyed man who was scrutinising her as if she was the latest curiosity. Who was rumoured to have a bad temper. Who was rumoured to always want to have things his way.

Fortunately, Johanna had business to discuss. She had asked the coach driver to return to the palace via a longer route that took them past the areas that were worst affected by the fires. Most severely burned buildings had been demolished and, with summer in full swing, those houses that were going to be rebuilt this year were progressing at a steady clip, though many building lots still lay empty. In one place a group of carpenters were replacing a bridge that had been burnt beyond safe use. Johanna explained how citizens had rallied together to pay the carpenters and how they were sharing houses so that the houses of everyone could be rebuilt. She explained how the shops and warehouses were surviving and how a fleet of canal boats had sprung up to ferry goods around the city that would otherwise be carried by wagons over the city's many bridges.

King William snorted. "It irks me how all that hardship is necessary because that old man gave all your money to that silly church. Did you ever find out what he hoped to achieve except a pile of burnt rubble?"

It was a remark as rude as it was apt.

"We can only guess about the king's motivations. King Nicholaos and Queen Cygna were both killed."

"Yes, I know. But would it be too hard to find out what the church did with all the money? That's what worries us from where we're standing. Because the Carmine family was not poor, and the church could easily have built a pretty stone building with their fortunes. One that didn't burn down." He gestured a large, hairy-fingered hand at the window. "They could have repaired all these things with that money. If the Church indeed got all of it and if the Carmine family truly has so little money left."

Johanna's cheeks flushed. "I'm sorry, but do you mistrust me?"

He laughed. "You have innocence written all over your face, little queen."

By the Triune, the rude boor!

He continued, "Let me give you a little hint. Royal families from as old a lineage as the Carmines have hundreds of years of experience in covering their tracks. The money you find in the coffers is rarely all there is. It is rarely even *most* of what they possess."

His attitude needled her. He was probably doing this on purpose to see how far he could go. She could dispute him and tell him that they had already looked everywhere and found very little. "Does this mean you want to tell me to look for that money before asking for your investment in our port? You're wrong about that. I don't want anyone's investment to solve our financial problems. As you can see, we're managing quite well. I want the money to build something we can all be proud of and to ensure lasting peace in this area."

King William threw his head back and laughed. That loud laugh of his hurt her ears and was getting very irritating, especially in a small space like this. It was as if he treated every question she asked as childish.

Johanna's anger flared. "If you truly believe that I'm stupid, then I can assure you that the meeting will be very short." By the Triune, she was trembling and sweating, and hardly dared look aside to see Father's horrified face, for surely he would be horrified.

King William's face became serious. "Let me be very serious with you. Your spunk amuses me. You're a merchant daughter having wedged herself into a fragile royal family who have made a lot of stupid decisions made worse by a run of rotten luck. But don't, for one moment, believe that you're ever going to be worth more than that child you're carrying. We are here because the concept of investment in dedicated quay space and warehouses interests us. For far too long, that harbourmaster with his exorbitant fees has annoyed our captains, not to mention your ridiculous taxes. The proposal that your men have drawn up is worth discussing. That's why we're here."

Johanna stuck her chin in the air. "For your information: *I* wrote a good deal of that plan. And I prefer if the plan was the main thing we discussed, not my status or my worth. And you're wrong about my worth, by the way. I will prove it to you."

He did not laugh anymore. Those steely blue eyes turned cold. "Do you really think you can be a match for a king in one of the oldest royal lineages in the known world?"

"I obviously don't have your experience . . ." —in being a pompous arse— ". . . but I've saved the crown, I've led my people into Florisheim, I've helped them ward off ghosts, I've freed them from magic, I've defeated a tyrant, so maybe yes, I can."

He nodded. "Challenge accepted."

Johanna returned his gaze, a little seed of triumph growing inside her.

CHAPTER 6

FORTUNATELY THE REST of the ride to the palace was short.

The coach stopped at the bottom of the palace steps where a guard of honour waited for the king. They were all dressed in smart Carmine livery. The marble steps they stood on were neatly swept and the entrance to the foyer with its marble columns had been scrubbed clean.

The herald announced the arrival of the king, and the soldiers lifted their trumpets, glittering in the sunlight. The fanfare echoed over the forecourt.

Hang all of King William's pomp. Those were her men, and they looked good and presented well, and she was proud of them.

A good number of citizens had gathered on the other side of the gilded fence and looked on while the party arrived. Besides their own, there were two other coaches, with the king's entourage and their luggage.

It struck her that, as ordinary Johanna Brouwer, she would have loved to see this. She would have stopped and watched, and told Father all about the extravagant clothing, and he would have sniffed and said that rich people had no sense of what money was really worth, or some such.

Now, she took Father's velvet-coated arm and walked up the stairs, chin held high.

A whole bevy of servants waited in the foyer, ready to take the king and his companions to the guest quarters. Apart from the foppish Earl, the king's entourage had alighted from the second coach and were just coming up the stairs.

As soon as they were in the foyer, Father fled to his study, with the excuse of having work to do, and it was left to Johanna to lead the party to their lodgings.

The guest quarters had gone through a complete cleanup in the last few weeks. The apartment consisted of a large sitting room in which the palace servants had collected a fine selection of furniture, with a bedroom off the main room. There were two large four-poster beds in that room, each with a luxurious bedspread and ornate curtains. Nellie had really worked hard to get the quarters in this state, and Johanna could see the little touches of Nellie's presence everywhere, from the little posy of dried flowers on the bed, to the way the curtains hung. And to think that Alexandre's bandits had used it as their camping room, and had even made fires in the corner.

The Earl immediately crossed to the window of the room. "You have a vegetable garden at the palace? My, you do things differently here." His voice was really annoying and Johanna wasn't sure whether he was interested or whether he wanted to mock her. "My husband is a keen gardener. I'm told it is a very relaxing pastime. Anyway, make yourself comfortable in this room. The maid will come around when the evening meal is ready."

And with that, Johanna could finally leave him.

While King William settled in the guest quarters, Johanna quickly ducked into her private sitting room before the evening's informal meal. Her feet were sore and she needed to lie down for a bit.

Father was also there, reading and writing up the last of his notes.

"That was . . . interesting," Johanna said.

"He'll be a difficult character to work with," Father said without looking up from his work. "He's not here to negotiate or to be cooperative. He's trying to provoke us. And succeeding admirably." He gave her a stern look.

"He was being condescending."

"Dear daughter, 'Condescending' is every king's middle name. Leave it. Ignore those remarks. He wants to poke you."

"Into doing what?"

"Getting angry at him so that he can show how much more superior they are in war?"

Because Anglia was superior, there was no question about it. Johanna sighed. "Let's hope he'll get along very well with King Leopold. They can both try to bluff each other under the table."

"Well, actually, it's King Benito you need to watch, because he seems to think that Lurezia can take on Anglia in the sea trade."

"Lurezia? They hardly have any ships. Not even half as many as we have."

"We don't have that many anymore."

"That's because they were all burned. We can still build ships. The Lurezians can't."

"I guess then you haven't heard the rumours that they bought blueprints off Li Han that show how to make the iron ships."

"I don't believe those rumours." Johanna spread her hands. "You don't need blueprints. Rinius has spelled it all out in his books. Once you can get over the fear of reading the books because they're banned, you can easily find this information. I know. I've seen it. Roald has the books. It's *building* the ships that requires skills that no one has mastered yet. This is what they were trying to do in the Guentherite brotherhood's summer residence. And they failed because they had a large explosion of bad air that, apparently, proves that Rinius is right about another matter of alchemy." She sat down on the couch, kicked her shoes off and put her swollen feet on the footstool. "Lurezia is controlled by the Belaman Church. They would not suddenly become interested in the very things that condemned Rinius to death: heretic sciences and alchemy."

"That's the other rumour: that the Lurezians are here to present the Belaman Church's viewpoint."

"The Belaman Church cast out the Church of the Triune. They have no say over us."

"Don't dismiss the Belaman Church so easily. They are a very old, very powerful and very rich organisation, who never took kindly to this new upstart church in Saardam that declared the Belaman Church's riches obscene and against the spirit of belief. Some will say that they should have been invited to this meeting, and they are probably still represented, though not in an official capacity."

"We're talking about business, not belief."

"The Belaman Church is up to its ears in the business of buying up land and farming and making money for its upper hierarchy. They're extremely powerful and can sink our project in the blink of an eye."

That was right. They could. In fact every single attendant to the meeting could possibly do so single-handedly.

The door opened and Nellie came in, red cheeked. "Oh, mistress Johanna."

"You look shocked, Nellie. Is anything wrong?"

"It's awful," Nellie said. "The king and that . . . foppish

little man are staying in the same room. Sleeping in the same bed." Her eyes were wide.

Johanna said, "What do you mean?"

"I heard rumours about that," Father said in a bemused voice.

Nellie nodded. "Isn't it outrageous, master? It's the same room where the shepherd's wife stayed. Imagine what he would have to say about this." She put teacups back into the cupboard and left the room again.

"Rumours about what?" Johanna asked after the door had shut behind her.

Father shook his head. "Sometimes I wonder what you did while you were out travelling with the duke's bandits."

"What does that have to do with it?"

"Well, were there any women there?"

"No. But . . ."

"Did they ever talk about women?"

"I don't get what you're talking about."

"I'm talking about bandits who plundered and could get whatever they wanted yet they were mostly uninterested in the women they found." He lowered his voice. "Because, you know, sodomy."

Oh. She had wondered what that meant and still had no idea what those men actually *did* to each other, and furthermore couldn't see how whatever it was that they did was hurting anyone. "Why does the church make such a big deal out of it?"

Father spread his hands. "Because it's the church?"

He dipped his pen in the inkpot and returned to his work, and Johanna left, feeling uneasy. Unless there was something going on that she didn't know about, she failed to understand why this *sodomy* thing was as worthy of preaching as bad magic. How many people did the practitioners of *sodomy* kill? Did they perform necromancy? Did they turn people into slaves under the very eyes of the church? Did they turn people into ghosts?

But maybe that was why the noble men considered her a weak queen: because she didn't see why certain things excited them so much.

Johanna could not possibly turn up even at the informal dinner in her utilitarian dress, so she heaved herself to her feet and went to the bedroom to get changed. She found Roald in the room. He sat on the bed, with his knees pulled up against his chest like an angry toddler, rocking to and fro. His face was set in a hard expression. A set of fine clothes lay on the bedspread next to him.

"Roald, what's going on?" Johanna sat next to him. He didn't reply, so she put her hand on his shoulder. His muscles were hard with tenseness.

"No," he said, his voice hard. He stared at the bedspread.

"I haven't asked you anything yet."

"No."

"Who asked you to do what?" It would be someone who had told him that he had to come to dinner, Father probably, in the time that Johanna had taken King William to his quarters. Father could be a little set in his ways. Not always very tactful, she had to admit. And yes it would be great if Roald could show his face at dinner, because it would make dealing with pompous men like King William and King Leopold so much easier.

"He said I had to dress up and behave like a real king. I don't like that man. I am the king and I can do exactly what I want." He stuck his chin in the air.

So it was probably not Father because Roald got on reasonably well with him, and Father would not have used those words. Whatever. Someone from the King's Council had told Roald that he should be there and Roald was digging in on the subject. "What if *I* told you that I'd like you to come? I don't really want to go either."

He looked at her, startled. "But you invited them."

"Yes, but that doesn't mean I like them." She was tempted to tell him what King William had said about her, but that would lead to all kinds of tangential discussions the she had no time for.

She said, "It's true. That can be our little secret."

"Hehe." He grinned. "I like secrets."

Yes, success. "But you know: they're only secrets as long as you don't tell anyone."

He looked disappointed. "But that's not exciting."

"No, but there is nothing exciting about this meeting. All these men are very boring and they're only here to see proof that we're poor and not coping with the situation—"

"That's not true at all. We are doing fine. We're fixing everything. We're not going hungry. I've got a garden full of beans that we can give to the poor people. And they get eggs, too. And carrots."

"I know." But the lack of crops being farmed outside the city because whole communities had been killed was something that would come to haunt them later in the year.

"Can I tell the guests about the garden?"

"I guess . . ." She wondered how that was going to go down with men the likes of King William, but it would be preferable to Roald talking about Rinius. "Come now." She pulled his arms loose from the tight grip around his knees. "I'll help you get ready or we'll be late."

She managed to get him dressed and then needed to get dressed herself. She told Roald to wait in the library for her to collect him. Nellie came to do her hair, red-cheeked and flustered.

"It's so busy, mistress Johanna," she said. "I scarcely know what to do with myself. I've spent all day on my feet organising the girls to do the rooms, and then I have to go and check to see if they did everything properly. Most of the girls . . . they're very keen and pretty, but they have *no* experience and no idea how to do rooms."

"Thank you for doing all that, Nellie."

"Oh, mistress Johanna, I wouldn't want to be doing anything else, but it *is* very busy right now."

Johanna had taken her place at the dressing table, and Nellie came with the jewellery box and combs, brushes and pins.

"Did you know that Loesie is back in town?" Johanna asked her.

Nellie's hands stopped combing. "Is she?"

"I met her at Father's sea cow barn."

"I really don't understand why that girl doesn't behave like everyone else. I'm sure she could come up here and you'd give her a proper room to sleep in. Why, mistress Johanna?"

"Because she's Loesie." And there was no other answer necessary. Because Loesie never did as you wanted or expected her to do. "She's got a friend with her." Johanna shivered at the thought of the girl's white eyes. "Apparently Duke Lothar is coming, too."

"Is he invited to the meeting, too?" Nellie looked slightly horrified. "I don't remember seeing his name on the guest list."

"Not personally, but he'll be welcome when he turns up." If anything, he and his bandits could make or break any agreement that would be made in Saardam in the next few days, either by attacking ships going upriver or leaving them alone.

Nellie replaited Johanna's hair and pinned it up. Johanna sat patiently through her ministrations. It promised to be a beautiful summer night, but one she wouldn't spend in the garden. Instead, they would be in the ballroom, where it got hot and stuffy on days like this, and where the servants would open the doors, which made things a little better, but which also let a lot of insects and sparrows into the room. And she would be tired, keen for it to end, and eating any of the rich food would give her the most dreadful case of heartburn.

She gazed wistfully out the window when she noticed that the water in the river bore several spots which appeared lighter than the surrounding water, *glowing*.

"Wait a moment," she said to Nellie, who had been getting ready with a bottle of perfume.

Johanna went to the window.

No, she had not been mistaken. Parts of the water glowed, and these patches appeared to be moving of their own accord, with the current, sideways, and against the current . . .

Nellie gasped, raising a hand to her mouth. "Oh mistress Johanna, are those. . . ?"

"Ghosts? I'm afraid so." She put a hand on her stomach, where the child was squirming and kicking. It was almost as if the little princess could feel the magic. Johanna could feel it, too.

Instinctively, she put her hand on the windowsill to see if any ghosts had come through this room, but all she saw was herself sitting at the dressing table, and Nellie coming into the room, followed by a young man . . . Frederik from the stables, she thought—and, goodness, Nellie! She snatched her hand off the windowsill.

"What?" Nellie whispered.

"I didn't know you liked Frederik that much."

Nellie exhaled a soft, "Oh." Her cheeks turned red. "Well, I . . . I guess I forgot that the windowsill is also made of wood, mistress Johanna. Sneaking around when someone in the house has a gift of magic is not easy."

"Don't be ashamed. He's a good man. We'll need all the

help we can find. He's good with horses, and we may just need horses. No person who has a good heart will receive any scolding from me. Saardam needs to stand united. I'm afraid Kylian did not come alone this time." Nor would he take defeat as an option.

CHAPTER 7

NELLIE CONTINUED doing Johanna's hair. While she pinned down recalcitrant locks and covered her creation with a jewel-studded hair net, Johanna thought that a lot of things suddenly made sense about Nellie's behaviour lately. For example, Nellie insisting on moving the dressing room furniture because it was "much nicer than the spare room stuff". She *knew* Johanna would see what she'd been up to, and had gone to great pains to remove the evidence, but couldn't remove the windowsill of course.

It also made sense how Nellie had been so happy recently. Nellie deserved a nice young man. But if anything, it drove home to Johanna that she and Roald weren't getting any closer to being a normal couple.

He could be silly, and they could laugh together. She would tickle him and sometimes they'd roll over the bed or the floor. It was fun but the times he'd please her were very few in between, and never seemed intentional on his part. Their coming together was a game more than an act of love, and of course he would never understand her.

She cared for him as a member of the family, like a

brother. But the relationship was all about him. From his perspective, there *was* no relationship. There was just him and the people who saw to his needs. She was just one of those.

Often, she wondered what it would be like to be dragged into a room, pushed up against the door and kissed silly, like she'd seen Frederik do to Nellie. She wanted to be carried to the bed and jumped on by a lover who knew that the act required two people to be satisfied.

When Nellie finished with her hair, Johanna went into the corridor where she met Father going in the direction of the dining room.

"Roald will be there," she said before he could ask. "I'll get him now."

"You look worried. Is anything wrong?"

Lots, but she couldn't talk about those things now, especially not about the ghosts and Kylian, or Loesie in the barn, or Duke Lothar. "No. Nothing that matters right now anyway. I'll be along soon, with Roald."

She could feel his gaze prick in her neck as she walked down the corridor. Father knew her well enough to know that something was up, and he wouldn't rest until he knew what it was.

Even though darkness had not yet come outside, no light reached the hallway other than from the candles burning in sconces. The light, adequate as it was to see where she walked, didn't reach in all of the doorways and niches. Johanna expected Kylian to come out of the shadows and sneak up behind her. She expected a cold hand over her mouth, and a stench of death and decay, or a stab of magic. Nowhere was safe, not even her own home.

Roald sat in the library, in one of the armchairs, reading his well-thumbed copy of Rinius. He looked so peaceful that she hated to disturb him.

"Come, let's go," she said.

She was sort of hoping that he would throw a tantrum and refuse to go, because once he had his head full of Rinius, he usually kept talking about the theories that had seen the author hanged in Seneza.

But he didn't. He simply put the book down on the little table next to his chair and rose. On the table was a sheet of parchment: the text of the speech she had written out.

Well, *that* was a much better sign.

He said nothing and took her arm as they left the library. Johanna was never sure what he thought of her other than that she was "his" woman and could get very defensive about her and Nellie, but sometimes she felt like he understood that there were certain things he really needed to do—even if he didn't want to do them—or risk people getting very upset with him. And he definitely didn't like that.

When they entered the ballroom, a lot of people were already standing around. They had not yet gone anywhere near the table, because the hosts of the occasion should be the first to be seated.

The herald at the door announced, "All hail King Roald and Queen Johanna of Saarland."

People cheered and clapped.

Johanna felt Roald's muscles tighten under the hand she held on his arm. He was staring ahead, avoiding the gazes of all those people at the table. And there were a lot more of them than she had realised.

Besides King William and his little assistant Earl Maximilian, the Anglian delegation consisted of two advisors and three businessmen. King Leopold had come with two nobles who were prominent Burovian businessmen, and the new Duke of Aroden was accompanied by his wife and three nobles. Baron Uti had also arrived. His son, of course, was not here, and neither was Li Han. But Johanna recognised some other familiar faces at the table. Fleuris LaFontaine had come with the baron, as well as Ignatius Hemeldinck. Both men wore dark velvet trousers and heavily frilled shirts such as Johanna had seen in the baron's castle. Neither of them showed any emotion when meeting her eyes, as if they had never seen her before.

Watched by all the guests, Johanna led Roald around the table to the two high-backed ornate chairs that stood there. He walked stiffly, like a puppet. Johanna had to help Roald pull out his seat, and a courtier rushed forward to help her. Drops of sweat glistened on Roald's forehead.

They sat down, and all the guests could take their positions as well.

"Welcome all," Johanna said into the oppressive silence. "I am deeply appreciative of your presence here in response to my invitation." She met King Leopold's eyes. He held lips pressed together. Clearly *he* disapproved of her being here or her having sent the invitations.

"The king will now say a few words of welcome."

Roald's face grew red.

He rose from the table, but had trouble standing because he didn't push the chair back far enough and the edge of the seat pushed into the back of his knees.

A courtier rushed over to pull the chair out of his way.

Roald stood frozen, staring at the table in front of him, while everyone was waiting for him to speak.

He stammered, "I . . . I . . ." His face grew even redder than it already was. He wiped sweat off his forehead.

Johanna turned to him and whispered under her breath, "Welcome to our home, distinguished guests."

He repeated her, haltingly and then went on with the text of the speech pretty much as she had written it. Welcoming the guests, hoping the meeting would be productive to cement a lasting peace between the countries in the region. His voice sounded a bit lifeless and rehearsed, but not bad enough to raise eyebrows. The speech touched on the reason why investment was necessary without mentioning the loss of the family's fortune to the Church, without mentioning the carnage and oppression by Alexandre and his men. It was a short speech, and contained little of importance. Ronald managed to get through with only a few minor stumbles.

When Johanna was reasonably confident that he'd get to the end safely—because Roald was much better than any person she had ever met at remembering written words—she studied the behaviour of the guests.

King Leopold would know of Roald's condition. His expression was blank, and he was drumming his fingers on the table, as if he was about to roll his eyes and ask for some "real men" to come and talk to him.

Baron Uti glared at Roald, but then again he always glared at everyone. He would be more than familiar with Roald's condition and looked ready to "ask the idiot to shut up."

Fleuris LaFontaine and Ignatius Hemeldinck looked bored. Ignatius was fiddling with a fork. Both men looked a lot older than when they'd been left behind in Florisheim. The dark velvet, trendy as it was in the baron's court, did not flatter either of them. Both men wore a lot of jewellery, so they must be doing well.

King William held his head cocked, as if he was highly interested in what Roald had to say. It was kind of eerie and strange in a way, as if he was the only one in the room who took Roald seriously.

Polite applause followed the speech, and when Roald sat down, Johanna gestured at the gaggle of servants carrying trays that had built up at the door so as not to interrupt the speech.

They now entered in a procession, depositing their heavenly smelling loads onto the tables. From the food, you would never know that Saardam's food stores were running low.

There were roast ducks and chickens and vegetables, some from Roald's garden. There was venison and an entire roast pig with the head still attached. There were cheeses and thick slices of warm bread, applesauce and butter, fruit and cream. A servant filled the glasses with cider.

Conversations started up around the table. Father had been in charge of seating. He had placed King Leopold next to Baron Uti and King William with his entourage on the other side of the table. He had placed Master Deim and himself next to King William, and the earl directly opposite Roald.

There were two other women at the table: Duke Aroden's wife and another woman who appeared to have come with Baron Uti, but whom Johanna had never seen before. She had ginger blond hair and a broad face. Maybe she was his daughter, although she looked a little old. Both of the women looked bored, and Johanna made a mental note to make an effort to talk to them.

For some reason the discussion turned to gardening, which the earl seemed to like. Roald spoke at length about his efforts. Had there ever been a dinner held in this room where royals discussed the matter of duck poo? The Earl liked roses, and they went on to discuss those. It looked like all potential disasters were temporarily averted.

Johanna leaned back into her chair. She was so incredibly tired and yes, the cook had excelled at producing the best, but the rich food gave her heartburn, as pretty much everything did these days.

She met Master Deim's eyes across the table. He and Father sat with King William and his entourage, talking, from what Johanna could judge, about tobacco and ships.

The king asked about the iron ships, and Father informed

him that Li Han was expected to attend the talks. The king knew Li Han, judging by the way he spoke about the eastern trader.

Johanna let the chatter wash over her. There was a lot of polite talk about the weather. Duke Aroden's wife had an annoyingly loud laugh. The woman with Baron Uti said little, and then only spoke to him while keeping her gaze fixed on the table. Occasionally she gave Johanna an angry look. Maybe that angry expression was just the way she normally looked.

Father and Master Deim now found something to talk about with the new Duke of Aroden, who, Johanna understood, was a brother of the old duke who had been killed by bandits. The new duke had lived in many towns in many countries, some of which Father or Master Deim had visited, and some they had not.

Somewhere after much of the food had been consumed, there was a big to-do in the foyer.

Another group of noble guests came into the hall, with, in their midst, a dusty-looking, darkhaired, dark-eyed man on the wrong side of middle age.

There were cheers and hullos all around the table.

The newcomer was King Benito of Lurezia, dressed in a travel cloak and sturdy riding gear. He was a hawkish character with a large nose and slicked-back hair. He came around the table where he greeted Johanna by kissing her hand. His moustache tickled her fingers. He smelled of horse.

Servants rushed in with extra chairs, and the newcomers found places next to King William. That was *not* where Johanna would have put him. Not Father, either, judging by the look on his face.

"Look at you, old codger," King William said. "Didn't think you'd make it."

"Deciding to take the road was an interesting choice,"

King Benito said. "The road is so badly rutted that we had to pull the coach out of the mire no less than three times. But the river is not safe anymore."

"What are you talking about?" King Leopold scoffed. "We came down the river without the slightest problem in the world."

"That's because you own all the bandit troops that make passage unsafe, my friend."

"I most decidedly do not!"

"Either you or that cousin of yours."

"Do you have a problem with me?" Baron Uti said, placing both his hands on the table, as if ready to get up to teach someone a lesson.

Everyone had gone very quiet.

In the silence, the blond, broad-faced woman said, "Do shut up, pa. He's just poking you with a sharp stick to see if you will jump. You don't have to perform on his command."

King William let out a long bellowing laugh. Earl Maximilian giggled like a girl.

Then the others started laughing as well, including Baron Uti, even if he cast his daughter a furious glance.

Neither Fleuris LaFontaine nor Ignatius Hemeldinck laughed.

Discussions around the table went on where they had left off.

Johanna felt like she was losing control over the meeting. All these important men knew each other much better than she knew any of them. Moreover, they didn't speak much to her, referring instead to Roald, who gave them silly replies. His cheeks were red and his eyes bright from the wine.

Any time he started speaking, he waved his hands and strained his legs as if about to climb on his chair and do a little dance.

Maybe she should just let them talk and go to bed early.

Let Father and Master Deim handle matters on her behalf. She probably worried far too much. Not only that, worrying achieved nothing, because it was not as if any of these men would change their behaviour because of her.

She was looking for a way to escape when King William said, in a loud voice. "Say, I've brought all of you a fine drop of gin. It would be nice if we could find a nice spot where were we can talk as men amongst each other."

A lot of the men made noises of approval.

"Yes! Let's go into the garden room," Roald said.

"There are no seats in there," Johanna said. Certainly, he couldn't be serious about having a drinking party over his sister's grave?

"Who needs seats?" King William bellowed. His cheeks were even redder than Roald's.

"I would," Johanna said. "But I get that I'm not invited."

"Pah, the women can retire to some dressing room and talk about women's things. Seems to me that you have a lot to discuss." He looked pointedly at her belly.

CHAPTER 8

JOHANNA BIT HER TONGUE.

By the Triune, that man made her angry. Somehow, he had managed to turn a civilised meal into a drinking party. She hated it that they were dragging Roald along. He did not normally drink, and they would have him under the table in no time. Who knew what damage he would do to her plans while he was drunk?

The men all got up and filed out of the room into the open doors of the garden room, where servants were hastily lighting lamps and dragging in a few chairs for those men for whom standing was going to be a problem.

Johanna remained at the table with the Duchess of Aroden and Baron Uti's daughter. Duchess Aroden gave Baron Uti's daughter a suspicious look and was rewarded with a scowl.

What a pair. Johanna couldn't possibly have picked two less compatible women had she tried. What in the Triune's name was she going to say and where would she take them? Idle women's chatter about clothes, children and artistic pursuits was not her thing. She couldn't imagine it was the baron's daughter's thing either.

Then she had an idea. Her old house used to have a smoking room where Father would sometimes take valued customers or friends. He would have tea brought up there while the men smoked pipes and pondered about life and other things not related to business. At her house, it was a little sunroom, jutting into the garden, with large windows, a table and a couch or two.

The palace had a similar room, even if it had not yet been included in the latest repair schedules. The room was, in fact, not too badly damaged. It was a little shabby but, since it was almost completely dark, no one would notice that.

A stream of servants moved into the ballroom to clean up the remains of dinner. Johanna stopped one of them and asked for tea and cakes to be brought to that little sunroom.

The woman said she would, and so Johanna asked her two female companions to come with her. She led them out of the hall into the foyer and then across the hallway of the unrestored office wing to this little room.

The windows were open and the soft night air that came in was laced with the scents of summer. An owl or some other bird of the night wailed in the distance.

Johanna bade the two women to sit.

"I am awfully sorry, but I don't remember your names," she said.

"I'm Carlotta Aroden," said the duke's wife.

Johanna said, "My mother was an Aroden. Her name was Sara."

"Oh, yes, I remember her. She was from the other side of the family."

A wealth of emotions hid under that slightly cool response.

Growing up in Saardam, Johanna had only ever seen

glimpses of the intrigue and rivalry between the two halves of that family and it was probably best not to delve into it.

She shifted her attention to the baron's daughter. "And your name is?"

"Natalya." She sounded peevish, but that could be a product of her heavy accent.

"I understand you are Baron Uti's daughter?"

She seemed to find that funny. "Ah, no. Baron would want that he has daughter. But he does not. I am daughter of Baroness Viktoriya."

"But I thought you called him 'pa'?"

"I did. Everyone calls him pa. But I am not his daughter." The expression in those widely spaced eyes was confrontational, as if challenging Johanna to ask who her father was. Johanna wasn't sure that she needed the complication of knowing this.

The servant woman entered with a tray from which she unloaded a plate of cakes and dainty biscuits, a teapot and cups onto the little table in the middle. She poured the tea and gave each of the women, starting with Johanna, a cup and a plate with one biscuit and one little cake.

Then she bowed and left.

"How long?" asked Duchess Carlotta, with a nod at Johanna's stomach.

"About another month."

"Oh, I remember how terrible it was with mine. I could barely move. It's admirable that you are here hosting us all."

The duchess, as she was happy to volunteer, had three children, all of them quite small, currently being looked after by her sister. She gave their names and ages, named their tutors—apparently having tutors was important—and outlined who would inherit which part of their land.

Johanna tried to listen, but found her attention waning. Natalya rolled her eyes several times.

Johanna tried asking *her* questions but she kept her answers short and clipped, and Duchess Carlotta would jump in with a flood of trivial matters that were not always related to the question.

Johanna tried steering the conversation away from the subject of children to the reasons the women had come.

Duchess Carlotta seemed to have come purely for reasons of entertainment. The children were too noisy, she needed time away from them, and oh did they know how much more pleasant the climate in Saardam was compared to the stifling humid summers in Aroden?

Natalya said very little. While Carlotta produced a flood of chatter, Natalya studied the room, eying the ceiling with its patches of peeling paint and the comfortable chairs that had seen better days but that had somehow survived treatments by Alexandre's bandits.

There was something chilling about that cold gaze from her strangely wide-spaced eyes.

Eventually Johanna could no longer contain her curiosity. When Duchess Carlotta fell silent because she was sipping her tea, she asked, "Can you tell me, then, Natalya, what your father's family is and how you came to live at the baron's castle?"

"My father is Count Hector."

Duchess Carlotta gasped. She put her cup down so suddenly that it almost fell off the table. "But that is . . . the magician of the Black Mountains." She turned sideways, leaning away from Natalya. Then she met Johanna's eyes. "He is said to kill his rivals with a single look, and kill sheep so he can drink their blood."

Johanna had heard some of the stories. One she remembered in particular was that the count stood up for people in a village who were the subject of mistreatment by landowners. He wasn't, by all existing evidence, a real count, since that required being of noble birth. He did, however, seem to be a real magician.

Natalya stuck her chin in the air. "Whatever is said of my father, he is not a peddler of evil. The same cannot be said for some other visitors to this palace."

Duchess Carlotta snorted. "Whatever are you talking about, child?"

"I am not a child. I am many times older than you, although you probably won't believe me."

Duchess Carlotta stuck her chin in the air. "You are one of those . . ." She spread her hands.

"Yes, one of those. The world is divided into those with magic and those without. Magic comes from the east and seeps through the land. Magic wants to insert itself into powerful families and powerful institutions. My mother and I went to the baron's castle when the signs came that the baron's newborn son was showing strong signs of magic. But the boy was already spoilt and the baron would not let us near him at important times."

All of a sudden, something else became clear to Johanna: the same division ran through the Aroden family. Her mother had never spoken of her home much. According to Father, she never even went home for the major celebrations, like weddings. Duchess Carlotta—married into the Aroden family —had casually dismissed her mother as being *from another part of the family* that she was unfamiliar with, probably unaware of the reasons why.

Magic. Because Sara Aroden had magic, she had been stripped of her noble title and entitlements and she had been allowed to marry a well-off but not noble Saarlander merchant. It had probably been a relief to the Aroden family when she died young.

She met Natalya's eyes, and saw in them that Natalya

knew, and that she spoke the truth about being much older than either of them.

"So," she said, hesitating. "Why did you come?" Her heart was thudding. She had expected this to be a boring discussion about children, tea and artistic pursuits.

Natalya turned her hand palm up. A little spray of sparks leapt from her hand.

Duchess Carlotta gasped and rose from her chair. "You have come here to sow evil amongst good people. Like that father of yours, and your stepfather and stepbrother. I would be done here and ask my husband to come home with me right now, if it weren't for poor Johanna, who has unwittingly unleashed this flood of evil on her city that has barely recovered from that last attack."

Natalya laughed loudly, in a way that reminded Johanna of King William. "Dear Duchess, I can assure you that *poor* does not describe this cunning little queen. Her machinations are why we are here. They are why we will sort out this magic in the next few days, even if the men think they've come here to talk about business and money." She laughed again. "All the forces of magic are gathering and won't leave until some of us have won, some of us are defeated, some badly wounded and some of us are dead."

"Don't talk like that. You sound like a man-wife."

"Whatever I sound like, it makes no difference when you're dead."

"This is scandalous. Are you making threats?"

"No, although you will not believe me. But petty concerns about what a woman *looks like* or *sounds like* are not important."

The Duchess huffed. "They should ban this filthy magic."

Johanna said, "Banning does not make it go away."

"Ban the people with magic. Put them in a fort and close the doors. Then we can go on with our peaceful lives."

Johanna rose.

"What?" Duchess Carlotta frowned at her.

"Show me your fort, because I'll only live in it if there is a good place for me and my child."

The duchess' cheeks coloured. She sat back down.

Johanna continued, "Magic goes where we have no control over it. Neither the king, nor the church nor any shepherd or holy father. People are born with magic like they are born with blond hair or with freckles. They can't help it."

Natalya nodded sagely. She was going to say something but at that moment a shout echoed from somewhere else in the building, accompanied by the sound of breaking glass.

"Oh, those men," Duchess Carlotta said. "They always drink too much and lumber about like idiots. Should we check to see what they're doing?"

"It is not drink," Natalya said. She was looking out the window and Johanna followed her gaze. A telltale pale glow hung in the garden.

The Duchess gasped, and raised her hand over her mouth. "But that's . . . that's . . ."

A ghost.

CHAPTER 9

JOHANNA MET NATALYA'S EYES.

"Ghosts are not common here?" Natalya asked.

Johanna shook her head. "I think your stepbrother has brought them. He is here. I haven't seen him yet, but I've seen his ship."

Natalya nodded. "He has brought all his unused souls and other ghoulish creations. They wander around feeling lost and trying to trick people into giving them more power."

"It's worse than that," Johanna said. "King Nicholaos hired the necromancer to resurrect his daughter. He was only partially successful and the princess' ghost hovers around, attacking unsuspecting citizens. She must be looking for her place of rest. The men are now having a drinking party over her grave."

Duchess Carlotta gave a little gasp. Her face looked very pale.

Johanna said to her, "If you're uncomfortable, feel free to retire to your quarters."

"Then what are you going to do?"

Natalya replied. "We'll see if any ghosts need warding off. It's not something I recommend for nice ladies."

The duchess straightened her back. "What do you think I am? You may think that I'm dumb and I'll need smelling salts at the sight of the merest little ghost, but I am the Duchess of Aroden and I protect good against evil. You may call our host Johanna cunning, but she is about to become a mother, and I'll protect her dignity and her child from the likes of you."

A man brandishing a sword now ran through the garden, and further shouts came from the garden room.

Johanna led the way back into the hallway, through the foyer, through the ballroom, where a couple of guards stood huddled in a group just inside the garden room door, looking frightened.

"Oh, Your Majesty," one of them, a young man, gasped. He was barely old enough to have a few hairs sprouting from his chin.

"What happened?"

"We didn't see all of it because we were guarding this door here, but all of a sudden there was this terrible scream and something smashed through the window."

"Did you check?"

He shook his head. "Our orders are to guard *this* door, Your Majesty. It could be a trick to draw us away."

His companion's eyes were wide. "I never go into that room unless ordered. You shouldn't go in there either, Your Majesty. It's haunted. I wouldn't want anything to happen to the little one."

"Our husbands and fathers are in there, so I'm going anyway." Johanna sidestepped them to the double doors that provided entry to the garden room. She was fuming. That was all they cared about: the heir to the throne.

King William's words came back to her. *You will never be worth more than the child you carry.*

Duchess Carlotta said behind her, "It strikes me that you may want to dismiss some of your guards, if they're as weak as that. If any of our guards said that to me, they'd be dismissed on the spot."

That comment hit Johanna in the gut. She hesitated with her hand on the door handle.

She was a weak queen indeed, one who allowed men with ulterior motives to run her life. Of course Duchess Carlotta was right.

But the guards were Johan Delacoeur's responsibility.

Then dismiss him, too.

Roald could do this. He had the power.

But wrecking people's livelihoods and making enemies out of reluctant friends was not her style. She appreciated Johan's experience, and believed that he would select better men if only he could find them. He was very old-fashioned and still needed to fully come around to the idea of having her in charge.

Dear Johanna, you are much too nice, Master Deim had said on many occasions. Usually, he was talking about the church, but it was something that he would say about Johan Delacoeur, because as a seasoned merchant, he never trusted anyone.

Not trusting anyone was something she had a lot of trouble with.

She opened the door to the garden room a crack.

A stifling waft of liquor-laced air came out.

Johanna peered into the darkness. The lights had gone out, and the only thing she could see were rectangles of moonlit garden through the windows directly opposite the door. A patch of light hovered in the garden, an ethereal figure in a dress, holding what appeared to be a lance at some-one's head.

By the Triune, how badly had these stupid men provoked this ghost?

Johanna pushed into the room, ignoring groans and other sounds in the darkness. She nearly tripped over someone's arm, then slipped on a wet patch—she hated to think what that was. It stank of liquor in the room, laced with a distinc-tive tang of vomit.

"Here let me help," Natalya said. She held her hand up. The shower of sparks that came from it cast an ever-so-faint glow by which Johanna could avoid the legs of another man passed out on the floor. She didn't try to see who it was, didn't want to know.

Weren't these nobles just disgusting? How long had she and the two women been drinking tea? And they had managed to get this drunk in that short period?

She reached the door to the garden.

A couple of people also stood looking outside, but she couldn't see who they were.

The ghost was slowly circling the man who lay huddled on the lawn.

"Who is that?" she asked.

A dry voice replied, "You shouldn't be here, Your Majesty. It would be harmful to the heir of the throne."

That sounded like Theo Kloostermans. Whenever had he snuck into this meeting? He definitely hadn't been at the dinner.

"Thank you for your concern, but I asked who that is. I can look after my own wellbeing."

"It is Shepherd Victor." Johanna recognised Master Deim's voice. And Shepherd Victor also hadn't been at the dinner. What was going on?

"What happened?" *Like, what are they doing here?*

"We were just minding our own business, and this . . . apparition came out of the ground while we were all talking and drinking—"

"Drinking mainly, by the look of things." Johanna said, and if she sounded peevish, then fine.

"It is what men do, Your Majesty," Theo Kloostermans said. "With all due respect. This is when deals are made."

"When everyone has passed out on the floor? Then it's no wonder that these men and their deals are all so stupid. Us women, cast aside for being *no more than the child you bear* were discussing real power." By the Triune, she was angry all of a sudden at all these stupid attitudes. "Anyway . . ." She undid the latch to the door.

Theo Kloostermans held his arm in front of her. "Don't go out there, Your Majesty. Think about the heir—"

"The heir is fine with this. Stop trying to control me, because you don't and you can't." Johanna sidestepped him. "I've dealt with this ghost before." Not that it had always ended happily. But she knew that she could control the ghost with her wood magic. The box that Li Fai had given her was in her study, but she happened to know that there was rake with a wooden handle leaning against the wall just outside the window, because she had seen Roald leave it there.

Johanna stepped onto the paved area outside the door. She found the rake, and went down the stairs into the old rose garden.

Once she had moved away from the palace, away from the talk of the men, she could hear the Shepherd's wailing voice in prayer.

Someone walked on the gravel path behind her. It was Natalya, of course, following her as a silent shadow. Duchess Carlotta came as well, following a bit behind Natalya. If nothing else, Johanna admired her determination. She must be frightened to death.

The ghost of Celine circled the figure on the ground.

The Shepherd was face down, on his knees, backside up, his hands clasped in prayer. He was crying, the words muffled in the grass.

Johanna remembered the vision she had seen when Li Fai had given her the box. It had shown her the Shepherd breaking down when trying to control the relic that was still trapped under the tree in the house where he and his wife used to live. The relic had been calling evil beings and foul forces into the church, and the Shepherd had been powerless to control them.

When she asked, Li Fai had said that the visions showed *possible futures.*

She shivered.

Johanna held the rake in front of her. Natalya stood next to her, holding out her hands. Duchess Carlotta had wrapped her shawl around her head, leaving just a small opening for her eyes, nose and mouth. The whites of her eyes showed with fear, but she didn't back down.

The ghost stopped moving, and cast her ice-cold gaze in Johanna's direction. She laughed, her mouth wide open.

The air she exhaled turned to ice, burning against the bare skin on Johanna's face and hands.

The lance in her hand fused with her arm and grew into a long tendril.

The ghost's other arm grew longer, too. Celine's hair fused into moving tentacles that looked like writhing snakes.

The Shepherd lifted himself on his knees. He balled his fists at the sky. "By the Holy Triune, Bearer of Evil, begone with you!"

The ghost ignored him, having found someone new to

play with. She floated closer to Johanna, walking about a hand's width above the ground without touching it. She wore the yellow dress that used to be the favourite of Celine's. Her feet were bare.

A feeling of cold magic went through Johanna's stomach. She raised the rake, willing the wood to start growing, but the rake's handle remained a rake handle, showing her distracting images of the garden in full daylight and Roald on his knees weeding the carrot beds.

Why didn't this wood grow in the same way it had grown when trapping Alexandre? That twisted tree had grown from a broom handle.

Because there had been many other people. Maybe there had been other people with magic who didn't know they had magic, or maybe the magic just needed other people to work, or—

The ghost was coming closer. The tentacles reached out for Johanna. She stumbled back, and almost tripped over the edge of a garden bed. She was so heavy and awkward, and a fall could be much nastier for the heir to throne than anything the ghost could manage to do.

Johanna's backside hit the hedge and she could retreat no further.

The Shepherd was yelling at the top of his voice. "Begone you devil, begone! The holy Triune with smite you to the seven hells."

The cold exhaled breath of the ghost bit into Johanna's skin. She squinted her eyes against it, continuing to wave the rake.

She willed it to sprout buds. She imagined the vines as they had grown from the broom handle. She imagined the tree as it had grown from Li Fai's wooden box, but the rake refused to obey.

Celine's ghost reached for Johanna's hand with tendrils of glowing ether. This close up, the ghost's face didn't resemble Celine at all. The face was skull-like, the eye sockets were empty, the nose two elongated slits, as if the flesh had rotted off. The hair writhed and twisted into knots. The mouth had no lips and pointed teeth. It opened, emitting a low hiss that made the hair on the back of Johanna's arms stand up.

Johanna was holed up against the hedge, which was too tall for her to step over. She had nowhere to go. She had tempted this ghost too often. This time, the ghost would win. The mouth opened further—

Then a female voice hissed foreign words that sounded like shards of glass slicing through fabric. A breeze whirled around the ghost, whipping up leaves and dirt. Johanna's skin stung with the warmth of it, after the icy cold of the ghost's magic.

The ghost froze.

The woman's words filled the night. Reverberant, sibilant, sonorous, the tone of her voice was everything at once. She stood with her hands stretched out. The woman was Natalya, of course.

The ghost let out a hiss of cold air that pushed against the warm breeze, but it couldn't manage to drive it away.

The ghost retreated past Natalya and the Shepherd. It floated backwards across the lawn and the garden beds, and before it reached the wall, it winked out and was gone.

Johanna lowered the rake.

Duchess Carlotta was staring at her.

Johanna wiped sweat off her face. She asked Natalya, "What was the thing you just said?"

"It is a simple spell for repelling ghosts. Ghosts are afraid if they have never heard it before. After a while, they get used to the spell and it won't work anymore. It was a gamble that it would still work on this ghost."

"Well . . . thank you."

"You should not go fight this ghost anymore. This is not a simple ghost. This is something more evil."

"It is the ghost of princess Celine, resurrected years after her death. It's Kylian's attempt at necromancy."

Natalya hissed. "We do not speak his name."

CHAPTER 10

SHAKEN AND FEELING SHIVERY, Johanna led the women back to the garden room, where a number of the men were standing at the top of the stairs, talking in groups. In the dark, it was hard to see who they were except for the tall one, who was probably King William. She recognised Master Deim's voice in amongst their chatter. He was saying, "The danger has gone now. We can all safely go to our beds . . ."

"Where is Father?" Johanna asked him.

A slightly stooped figure detached from one of the groups and enveloped her in a hug. "Please, Johanna, will you never do that again? I thought it would kill you."

"I'm all right," Johanna said. She shrugged off his concern, because admitting that she had thought the same would bring all sorts of unwelcome thoughts. "Where is Roald?"

"Inside. He didn't see the ghost of his sister."

"Did you shelter him from the sight?" That was surprising. Roald tended to be curious.

"He's . . ." Father hesitated. "He'll be all right."

Johanna wasn't sure she wanted to know what was behind

that evasive reply. The air that wafted out of the open doors into the room stank of liquor. Roald never drank. That was probably as much as she needed to know.

Someone had lit a lamp inside the room, and by its light Johanna and the two other women picked their way between glass, a fallen chair and messy patches on unmentionable substances across the room. She spotted at least three men asleep on the floor. No one she recognised.

The little Earl was at the table that the men had dragged in from the ballroom, pouring himself another drink. He hefted his glass when Johanna passed, and giggled. "Cheers." His cheeks were bright red. "I will . . . will drink to . . . the van—vanquishing of the goat—er, ghoaf—ghost! Hic."

"Disgusting," Duchess Carlotta said in a low voice behind Johanna, and for once, Johanna agreed wholeheartedly with her. She also noted that Duchess Carlotta made no attempt to find her husband.

"They're happy now, but they won't feel so good in the morning," Natalya said.

Duchess Carlotta snapped, "And they won't want to get out of bed, and they'll be complaining about their heads all day."

There was clearly some backstory to this remark, and Johanna thought it wise not to ask any further. Duchess Carlotta was right, and it was annoying.

Tomorrow morning was the day that Father and Master Deim had planned to take the visitors around the city to show them the possible sites for building new quays and warehouses. It was an important day in the program and she'd wanted the men to be alert and asking questions, not worrying about their heads.

And then a thought: King William thought that she was just a little woman, worth only as much as the heir she could produce. Was he deliberately trying to distract all the guests?

By the Triune, he wouldn't do that, would he?

In the ballroom, she found the group of terrified guards in the same position as they had been when she came through. Seeing them there made her angry, too. Had they done anything to prove their worth?

One of the men gasped. "Your Majesty! You're back."

"Yes, I am. You can now go in there. The ghost is gone so you don't have to be afraid anymore. It is quite safe. While I've been doing your job, I wonder why I pay for you when you're standing out here being scared, like a bunch of adolescent girls. Go inside and help clean up the mess. Put a halt to this raucous party. Drag these men to their beds where they belong. Take away their liquor."

The guard flinched. "Yes, yes, Your Majesty." He bowed.

"Then don't just stand there. Do it!"

The men scurried off.

"Idiots," Johanna said in a low voice. She really must talk to Johan Delacoeur about it. She knew what he would say: that it was hard to get good men, and no doubt it was. But better training cost nothing. He'd better explain to her why he hadn't yet started that training.

"Sometimes you need to scare the men," Natalya said. "Otherwise they will just do whatever they want. Men are stupid. They do not think."

Johanna could definitely agree with that. "This makes me angry. These men called up Celine's ghost by having the party over her grave. It was their fault."

"They will always do what they want, because you're a woman and they won't listen to you. But we rule the world of magic and ghosts. You wanted to know the reason why I came with the baron. I didn't tell you because I first wanted to see if I can trust you. Now I think I can. Come. It is high time that we talk about this." And she took off across the foyer.

Johanna followed Natalya down the stairs that led to the old servants' quarters, with Duchess Carlotta close behind.

On the way down, Natalya told her, "The pull of magic is very strong in this city. Everyone who has even the smallest gift of magic will want to travel here. They will make up an excuse to go, but their mind is pulled here and they cannot say why they suddenly have to visit relatives they haven't cared about for years. They are drawn here because the magic lines have broken to the surface. They are virgin lines that have never been seen before. Everyone wants to draw from their power."

Johanna remembered Duke Lothar talking about magic lines in his estate. She remembered the living tunnel of trees.

"We never had magic in Saardam."

"No, that's right. The lines must have shifted. Magic things must have happened that have brought the lines to the surface. Or maybe the magic discovered this virgin, empty place, and all the types magic are fighting to own it."

"Magic events . . . We trapped Alexandre's spirit in a tree, and we did the same with a relic from the Church."

"Those are evil things. I can feel them, and I have been around a lot of bad magic. Those vessels of evil have not been defeated. They're struggling against their tree prisons. Give them half a chance and they will escape. I can think of several people who would love to give them a hand."

She didn't need to name names. Kylian, Baron Uti, maybe even King William would be happy to have his greatest rivals in the sea trade occupied with something other than seafaring. Then he would pounce, snag Li Han's business and the iron ships.

They arrived at the bottom of the stairs.

This was another part of the palace that had been relatively unaffected by the carnage upstairs, but that was also in need of repairs and freshening up. Originally, these were servant quarters. At the moment, there were not enough servants in the palace to fill up all the rooms, and this was where the extra influx of less important visitors had been put up: any of the travel companions who had no ship to sleep on, and who would not stay in their master's rooms.

So far, the Lurezian party was the main one that had come overland, and Lurezian was the main language spoken in the passage, by the men in the livery of King Benito who stood talking in groups and who greeted Johanna with bows when she came past.

Like many basement corridors, including the one in her familiar old house, the basement had a low ceiling barely high enough for the tallest of men. The kitchens were here—on the other end of the hallway, as well as the servants' bedrooms.

The hallway was quite wide and well-appointed, with little benches along the sides, as well as some statues and ornamental vases that had probably been received as presents by King Nicholaos and Queen Cygna and had been deemed not good enough to be displayed upstairs. Johanna remembered walking through the storeroom containing all this material, dusty and soot stained but strangely untouched by the bandits who had occupied and plundered the palace. They must not have known anything about art because they had left many priceless items: paintings and vases, gold-rimmed plates and carved statues.

Natalya knocked on a closed door at the end of the passage.

A young woman in a maid's dress opened and spoke to Natalya in a language that Johanna didn't recognise. She looked at Johanna and dropped into a curtsy, then she stepped back, opening the door further.

Johanna went inside. It was dark in the room, which was a

typical servant's room, with enough space for a bed, a chair and small table and a clothes rack.

A nun rose from the chair, in a habit that covered her arms and went all the way to the ground. Her cap and veil were white and blue, her habit dark blue. Johanna had no idea what order that represented.

She curtsied. "It is good to see you, Your Majesty." She spoke with a southern accent.

The woman's face was unfamiliar, if perhaps a little too well-fed to be in a monastery.

The woman went on, "Thanks so much for seeing me at this time of the day in your condition. Do take my seat, Your Majesty."

Johanna wanted to protest. She got a little sick of situations when people treated pregnancy as a debilitating disease. Farmers' wives worked in the field right up to the moment their children were born. But this game of being the most polite in the room was going to go on forever, so she sat, and let the nun take place on the bed. Natalya shut the door, cutting off the view of the corridor and a couple of curious maids standing there.

Then there was a small sound, and Johanna saw that the nun hadn't been the only one in the room.

At her foot of the bed stood a bassinet with an infant.

That was . . . odd. Nuns didn't marry, they were married to the church. Any "fallen" nun who had a child wouldn't be allowed to stay in the order, let alone travel with a royal party of any kind dressed in a habit, while bringing her infant.

Unless . . .

The nun gave another little bow. "My name is Francina. You might have heard about me. I have joined the Sisterhood of Forgiveness recently."

"There is only one Francina I've heard of." But certainly

this woman couldn't be the same person as King Benito's latest wife?

She nodded, her eyes glittering. "He chose me, because I was a widow and I had two children by my first husband."

King Benito had succession problems, Johanna remembered, and that might have been the reason for such an odd choice as a wife. But why the nunnery and why wasn't she upstairs with her husband?

Francina reached out for the infant in the bassinet, who was fast asleep. The prince or princess was wearing a little bonnet, which Francina pushed down. The infant's hair was fox-red.

Not the king's obviously.

Johanna felt cold. The child inside her squirmed. She looked from Natalya to Francina to Duchess Carlotta, who was frowning and didn't appear to understand the implications.

Johanna whispered, "Is this. . . ?"

Natalya nodded. "The necromancer is spreading magic through all of the western lowlands by means of his children. It doesn't matter if the woman is a princess or a farmer's daughter, if she is married or not, if she is young or old, if she comes to his bed because she wants it, or if he has to rape her. Many infants are born that are his."

"Yours, too?" Francina asked, meeting Johanna's eyes.

Johanna looked down. "I'm not sure."

"Yes," Natalya said. "I can feel it. Here." She put her hand on her chest.

Johanna's cheeks burned.

"There are others. Princess Maribelle of Burovia has little girl. There is no father. Queen Margit of Montania has little boy, the heir to the throne. He is eight years old and quite possibly the oldest of all the necromancer's children. They are everywhere."

By the Triune, this was also what Loesie had been talking about, but from the perspective of the poor farmers' daughters who, cast out and frightened by magic, ended up on her farm. "What is he trying to do?"

Duchess Carlotta was looking on, her face pale.

"Are any of your children the necromancer's too?" Francina asked her.

Duchess Carlotta gasped. "Heavens, no." Her cheeks went red.

"He bewitched a lot of us, so there's no shame."

"Well," the duchess huffed. "That would not be an excuse in the eyes of my husband. If I said anything of the sort to him, he'd accuse me of seducing another man and being unfaithful."

"Pah," Francina said. "While being unfaithful themselves?"

"Husbands are useless," Natalya said. "They sleep, they get drunk, they act like they are important. They are not."

Francina nodded sagely. "My husband kicked me out. He allowed me to come here, because he is still hoping that the boy will turn out to be his son. He's not. Husbands try to control our lives, but they can't."

Duchess Carlotta didn't look too sure but eventually nodded as well, her face set. She repeated, "Husbands are useless."

"I cannot blame my husband for anything," Johanna added. "But his condition means that he does not help me at all. He is not interested in anything other than gardening and horses."

Francina asked, "Does he even . . . you know how to do it?"

"He does. He's not terribly interested anymore."

"If I were you, I would take a lover. Do you have one? Or more than one?"

"I don't," Johanna said.

"Well, that's a pity. As long as you're with child, there can't be any unfortunate consequences."

"Oh!" Duchess Carlotta exclaimed. "Your talk is really quite scandalous, for a nun. What sort of order is the Sisterhood of Forgiveness?"

Johanna had a feeling what was going on. "This isn't a real order of the Belaman Church, isn't it? I have never heard of the Sisterhood of Forgiveness."

"Oh, it's a real order, but not one that the Belaman Church agrees with. The order helps the women who have been unfortunate, who have fled from their husbands, whose husbands have cast them out or have run away, leaving the wife with the children and without money. The mothers take the habit as protection, and the children live in the convent."

What an excellent idea.

Francina continued, "Magic is very often the reason that the women were cast out. I started to notice a lot of children with red hair, all born of noble women. Their stories were all similar: they were seduced by a handsome red-haired stranger who did not mention anything except his name. Few know that he is the son of Baron Uti. For myself, I'm not ashamed of what I did. My parents brokered the marriage, but King Benito is a smelly old man, much more interested in horses than in people. He never gets violent when he's drunk, but he drinks so much that he doesn't get it up, if you get what I mean. I wasn't like some innocent noble girl. I know what's required to make an heir, and he can't do it, simple as that. He'll never have an heir. He knows that, and he wants the little boy to become his heir anyway, because otherwise the throne would go to his nephew, and King Benito hates his brother. So that's why I'm here. He wants me to take off the habit and pretend the boy is his son. I'll look after the boy, but I'm not going to pretend to be his wife and deal with his filthy habits anymore. But he is so afraid that something will happen to his heir that we had to come on this trip."

Magic. This was the thing that Natalya had been speaking about. Making up excuses to visit Saardam. That would have been Loesie's excuse as well.

A chill made the hair on the back of Johanna's arms stand up. All these people were here because of the magic she had unleashed.

CHAPTER 11

JOHANNA WOKE UP, her heart thudding.

It was dark in the room. Pale moonlight slanted in through the window, silvering the cabinet with the water jug and the bedpan.

Johanna lay back on the pillow, waiting for her breath to calm, wondering what it was that had woken her and given her such a fright.

She remembered leaving Francina's room in the servants' corridor quite late. Upstairs, it looked like the raucous drinking party had continued as if Celine's ghost had never been there. Clearly the two young guards had been unsuccessful at putting a stop to it. She had peeked into the room, but the stench of liquor and vomit had been even stronger than before, and she had simply decided to go to bed alone.

There had been a dream, she remembered vaguely. Something in which the gnarled tree in the market place came to life and started strangling people.

In the dream, she'd been leaning into the wind, gazing at the tree, while people rushed past in the market place.

Johanna was the only one who appeared to have noticed

the mangled and bloody body of Johan Delacoeur in the branches.

As the tree had dropped Johan's lifeless body at her feet, a throbbing red light had risen over the roofs of the city, coming from the Shepherd's house . . .

A stab of magic had gone through her, knotting into a hard ball in her stomach, making it glow from within. It wasn't painful exactly, but gave rise to a sensation of pressure of something that needed to get out.

She sat on her straight-backed chair in the ballroom, and all the men were looking at her.

Helena was in the room, yelling at her, "Push like you've got to shit really badly and you've been waiting for days to get it out."

Johanna wanted to say, "Not here," but she had no voice.

The child was coming and she was not ready for it. The meeting hadn't finished, they hadn't agreed on anything, and—

Then she woke up, gasping for air.

Her heart had calmed somewhat. She reached next to her, and found that the bed was empty. By the Triune, where was Roald? She sat up, but it was too dark to see if he had been in the room at all.

Johanna pushed herself from the bed to use the bedpan. It took a long time these days, and the cold edge of the metal bit into her legs.

The window stood open a crack, but she couldn't hear any sounds that indicated that the drinking party was still going.

Johanna found her slippers, pulled on the only dressing gown that still fit her—it was Father's—and waddled to the corridor. Ouch, her feet were so sore these days.

It was quiet in the hallway as well. The door to King William's guest quarters was closed, and when she listened at the door, she could make out the sound of snoring.

Now she was getting really worried. Where *was* Roald?

A young guard called Dirk—like Father—stood in the guard station in the foyer. He bowed when Johanna approached. The light from the oil lamp showed his surprised expression.

"The king?" he asked, his eyes wide when Johanna asked. "I wasn't on duty. I haven't seen anyone come this way since I started. It was all quiet, the other men said."

Seriously, what had those young guards been drinking? "Let's go and check it out."

The garden room was deserted. The floor had been cleaned—at least the part that Johanna could see in the pool of light from Dirk's torch—the glass removed and bottles and cups taken away.

There was no sign of Roald.

"When did you last see him?" Dirk asked.

Johanna had to think about that. It had been at dinner, because even when she came in here, after the Shepherd had broken the window, Father had told her that Roald was fine but that it was probably best if she didn't see him.

Probably he'd been blind drunk. Probably he had felt ill. Likely he had realised that she or Father would not be impressed.

What did Roald do when he thought she would be angry with him? He hid somewhere. In the garden usually.

"Come with me," she said, and crossed to the doors that opened onto the terrace.

The Moon had moved to bathe the western side of the palace in a pale glow that was bright enough to make out paths and hedges. Johanna grabbed the rake, just to be sure, and set off for the little gate that connected the old rose garden with the private garden where Roald grew his vegetables.

And there, something was definitely happening. A dark-clad figure was climbing out the window of her study. Now she realised what had woken her up: the breaking of glass.

Dirk yelled, "Stop, intruder!"

The man dropped himself out the window and ran through the garden. Dirk went after him.

When he had vanished, Johanna realised there was a second figure in the garden, on the path between the beanstalks and the carrots. He sat on his hands and knees, coughing. No, retching.

Johanna knew who that was. "Roald!"

She ran to him.

He coughed and coughed.

"Stop it. Calm down." He stank of stale liquor.

"He was . . . trying to break . . . into your workroom." He slurred his words. "I tried to . . . stop him."

She bent over, putting her hand on his shoulder. He felt cold and was shivering. Who had left him alone so that he could have wandered into the garden? Why had no one seen to it that he went to bed?

He coughed, bringing up nothing more than slime. He rocked from side to side on his hands and knees.

Dirk came back into the garden. "He was too fast."

"Did you see who it was?"

"Unfortunately not."

Johanna didn't think it could have been Kylian. She would have felt it.

"Take him inside." She nodded at Roald who still sat on his hands and knees, and let out a large wet burp. By the Triune, if she could play a trick on King William, she would. This was disgusting. "Make sure that someone washes him and puts him in bed."

Dirk nodded.

Johanna hoped that he wouldn't ask Nellie, but he'd go to

one of the maids instead. Nellie didn't deserve to have to deal with this.

Johanna needed to check her study. She lit a lamp from the firebox in the grate and walked around holding the light aloft.

The place was a mess. Glass and other rubbish crunched underfoot. Books and papers lay strewn everywhere. The ink had fallen over, leaking onto the rug.

Was anything missing?

The drawers that contained money were closed, and indeed the money was still there.

Then she lifted the lamp to the shelf where she kept Li Fai's box.

It had sprouted roots that covered most of the shelf.

Johanna gasped.

She reached out for the box. A spray of magic enveloped her hand. As she touched the wood, the roots evaporated, the box came loose from the shelf and it returned to its usual appearance.

The wood showed her a flash of magic too bright for her to see anything else. When she opened the lid, the little tree unfurled itself as it usually did. But the leaves seemed unusually bright and it was as if they *trembled*.

CHAPTER 12

JOHANNA'S HEART THUDDED like crazy. Someone had tried to attack the box.

That box was the symbol of her developing magic. She needed it. The box connected her with Li Fai. Apart from the tree, it contained memories.

She knew for certain: Kylian was stalking her and waiting to make his move. He was not interested in talk and civilised meetings. He would use magic. He probably wanted the box to cripple her ability to fight against him, maybe even to free Alexandre's spirit and the Church relic's magic from the tree. Kylian did not have wood magic, but he had brought all the magical tools that he had. He had brought Celine's ghost and a flood of other ghosts that would frighten the citizens—who were unused to magic—so much that they would either run or hide.

Last time, he had sent Alexandre with men and animals. Alexandre had been defeated, so this time, he had brought a magical army. Saardam had no ability to fight this invasion.

There was no time to waste. She should see Li Fai—rumours be damned—and also Loesie, to warn them. She should ask Loesie to call whatever assistance she could muster into the city. She should find Duke Lothar. He would not want to be found, but she could use her magic to track him down. The longer she waited to do this, the more time Kylian had to set up his plans.

But, first, she needed him to check if her box had been damaged or compromised, make sure it was still all right to use it.

Johanna went to change into her clothes. The dressing room looked out over the east, and a faint glimmer of daylight coloured the sky over the roofs of the city.

She had taken her dress out of the wardrobe and was wondering how to do up the lace when Nellie came in. Her eyes widened. "You're not going out right now, mistress Johanna?"

"Sadly, I am. Help me get changed."

Nellie started tying up the lace at Johanna's back. "But why, mistress Johanna? What could you possibly want to do at this time of the day?"

"I could tell, but you'd be horrified, so I won't."

"Well, *that* is certainly reassuring."

"I think there is a plot being cooked up for another occupation of the city."

Nellie gasped. "Why ever would you think that? The kings are all here to talk to you."

"A *magical* occupation."

Nellie took in a sharp breath. "But Kylian is not even here."

"He is in Saardam. I can feel him. I've seen his boat."

Nellie's face showed an expression of horror. Nellie knew all too well about the persuasive powers Kylian possessed. Johanna had always wondered what had happened between him and Nellie in Duke Lothar's garden, and now knew what *would* have happened had she not looked out the window and seen the two in a very friendly chat. It seemed that Nellie was lucky to have escaped the fate of so many girls.

She put on her cloak and left the room. It might be getting light outside, but it was still very dark in the corridor. A group of people, one of them with a torch, was coming into the end of the hallway. She presumed that these were the guards and servants with Roald. She felt guilty for not looking after him. Poor Roald. He really couldn't help that King William had enticed him into drinking far too much. Roald couldn't make those kinds of decisions for himself.

"Your Majesty?" Anton was on duty in the foyer, and he was surprised to see her.

"I have to go out," Johanna said. "I will need the coach and horses."

He nodded. "I will see to it." And he went out the main doors to the stables to rouse the coach driver.

Good old Anton. *He* did as he was ordered without questioning. He offered to help her, protect her, and was always there for her.

Johanna waited on the little bench in the foyer. The soft noises that echoed through the hallway indicated that somewhere in the palace people were getting up, ready to cook and clean. Soon enough someone would come up here to ready the table for breakfast, although the distinguished visitors would probably not be in the mood for it for several hours. She pulled the hood of the cloak over her head, unwilling to be recognised, just in case.

Anton came back. "The coach is ready."

Johanna followed him outside, where it had gotten significantly lighter. The coach stood at the bottom of the stairs with the two white horses.

After days of nice weather, storm clouds were rolling in and squally gusts of wind exposed the silvery underside of the leaves on the willow trees. Somewhere in the distance lightning flashed in the clouds. The air smelled humid.

"Where to, Your Majesty?" the coach driver asked. He held the horses' reins tightly. The animals were tossing their heads, manes flying in the gusty wind.

"The eastern trader's ship."

He nodded. Like Anton's, his face remained blank.

Anton helped her into the coach and while she settled on the familiar bench, he climbed up on the driver's seat. The driver whistled and the coach jumped into motion.

Not questioning their orders, that was how guards and servants were supposed to react. Not to argue, or let their own feelings or curiosity come through. She really should raise the subject of training with Johan Delacoeur. She had so much to learn about how to be a successful ruler that people would respect. Sadly, being kind or gentle wasn't one of those things. People took advantage of rulers who were too nice. Girls were always taught to be nice, so they were more susceptible to being taken advantage of.

The coach made its way through the city by the grey light of the early dawn. The only people on the streets were servants and merchants, hidden in the collars of their cloaks against the squally wind. They turned right onto the quay. The ships in the harbour bobbed on the choppy water, rigging and flags flapping. At King William's ship, a couple of deck hands were securing a couple of barrels around the foremast to stop them rolling around the deck.

The coach stopped at the mooring position of Li Han's iron ship.

Anton jumped off the driver's seat and came around to open the door. "Your Majesty, are you sure this is the place where you wanted to go? There is no one here."

"I'm sure, thanks." She took his hand to climb down the awkward ladder.

The wind made a lot of noise. Rigging flapped, hulls creaked. Unspecified things banged and squeaked. Most of the ships were visibly moving on their moorings. Except Li Han's ship. It lay as still as ever. Johanna glanced up at the smooth, dark metal side that loomed over the quay.

Johanna stopped at the bottom of the gangplank. "Li Fai!"

Her words were lost in the wind, so she called louder, "Li Fai, I need to talk to you."

She listened.

Maybe they were all asleep and would not wake up.

But then the sound of footsteps rang through the hull, followed by the unmistakable quacking of ducks. At least someone was awake.

"Johanna!" Li Fai stood at the top of the steep gangplank. "What are you doing here?"

"I need to talk to you." Johanna's voice was almost blown away by the wind. A lock of hair came undone from the bun and swept over her forehead.

Li Fai came down. He held out his hand. "Come inside. It's going to rain."

Johanna put her hand into his. His grip was warm and strong, and he pulled her easily up on the deck. She had only been here once before. Father and Master Deim had mostly dealt with Li Han, but Johanna had always kept herself a little distant, for fear of rumours.

How silly that seemed now. She should have come much earlier, to set up lessons for children with magic.

The ducks all bunched together in the corner of their cage, quacking, poking their beaks through lattice that was made out of some kind of twig.

"They're hungry," Li Fai said when he noticed her looking at them. "The deck hand will come soon to feed them."

Johanna followed him across the deck to the side of the

main cabin. A burly guard in leather armour watched them from above.

Li Fai opened a door and gestured Johanna into a spacious cabin that looked like a study, with a table in the middle, silk paintings strung on frames, shelves around the walls that contained jars of samples.

A couple of lights burned around the cabin, spreading a warm glow.

Li Fai indicated a little bench for her to sit on, and she did, enveloped in the nutty scent of spices.

He sat on another. "What is the matter?"

"I have come to warn you. Tonight, someone broke into the palace. I think he tried to steal my magic box."

"I know," he said. "I could feel a disturbance through my art. Show me the box."

She took it out of her purse. Held up in the palm of her hand, it looked very much like it usually did. Li Fai reached, touched with the tips of his fingers and withdrew his hand like he'd been stung. He took in a sharp breath. "The art is very strong."

"What does that mean?"

He shook his head. "I don't know. It feels like . . . the box defended itself when someone tried to imbue it with evil."

"Did he succeed at all?"

"I can't be sure. I'm but a small peddler."

"What about that large dragon of yours?"

"The dragon is not that brave. He wants to stay in his box. He doesn't like the feel of this man's art. The dragon can be a real coward."

Johanna couldn't help but laugh at that.

His face remained serious. "I'm speaking the truth. I'm not all that you hope me to be. I hate to disappoint you."

"You helped me defeat the relic."

"Your tree did most of that, and the relic was but an

object."

"A strong magical object."

"Yes, but I fear that you give me too much credit."

The expression in his eyes was sad and very serious. What did Johan Delacoeur usually tell her? *The best generals are highly aware of their own shortcomings.*

She let a silence lapse. It would be handy if he had all the answers, but then again, if he did, this situation wouldn't exit, because someone would have dealt with Kylian long ago.

"I'm sorry," she said in a low voice.

"There is no need for you to be sorry."

"There is. I assumed that you knew everything. I hoped that you could tell me how to defeat this evil, but it's not a thing one person can do. I just saw that in the garden with Celine's ghost. I should not have assumed that you are the answer to all my problems." Some problems, maybe, but those were probably best not mentioned.

"Can I still use the box, or do you have another box I could use?"

He shook his head. "Sadly, it doesn't work like that. The box is not easily replaceable. You will have to cleanse it."

"Do you know how to do that?"

"No. Except I know it's not easy."

"Can you help me?"

"Helping is always a good thing."

She went on to tell him all she knew about magic, including about Kylian's magical children and the women downstairs.

A deep silence followed her words. His throat worked as he swallowed. His gaze wandered from her eyes to her stomach and back again. "You shouldn't trust me blindly. How do you know what machinations my father has in place?"

"Your father, yes, I realise that. He has a business to run

and will make decisions accordingly. Trust doesn't come into it in the same way it exists between, say, friends or relatives."

He met her eyes. Blinked. Said nothing. Johanna's heart thudded. Any moment now he was going to tell her that she acted inappropriately, or he was going to say something that put her down as a stupid woman or shattered her wish.

He licked his lips. "Well . . ." And a moment later again, "Well . . . I could try to help you. I don't know how much good it would do, but—"

"Thank you." Johanna almost choked up inside. She had spent so long looking for a court magician without the slightest success. She might not want to give Li Fai that title, but his assistance was so much better than anything she had before.

A ghost of a smile went over his face. "With my little knowledge, I would say we would first need to . . . secure the spirits in the trees to make sure that no one can easily set them free."

Johanna frowned. "Shouldn't we should protect the kings first?"

"They can look after themselves."

"But the ghost is already in the palace."

"If they don't have the art and don't disturb the ghost, it won't harm them."

"That's easy to say. The Shepherd was trying to chase it off with prayer. It took exception to that." When ghosts wanted to start throwing things, there was a need to do something.

"If the shepherd left the ghost alone, it would not harm him. The palace and the stupidity of those men is not our main concern."

"It is mine, because if anything happens to any of my guests . . ."

"It will be many times worse when the spirits escape from

their tree prisons. I suspect that the necromancer is here to free his creations. By tampering with your box, he hampers your powers. He could probably sense the presence of the box, and wanted to render the power harmless before he makes his move."

"Can we stop him from reaching the trees?" One was in the market place, the other hidden in a house that was now abandoned. Both were easy localities to visit in a disguise and have no one notice it.

"We could try to put a ward around the trees so that we are warned when someone comes in—"

Johanna rose. "That sounds like a good idea. Let's do it now." She remembered Sylvan putting wards around the campsite at night when they were in the forest. "Do you know how to put wards?"

"Yes, but . . . I haven't done that for a long time. The spirits here are different. I may need someone else—"

"I'll come. We'll need to hurry, though."

He frowned. "There will be people in the marketplace already. Nothing will happen during the day. Spirits are active at night. We can come back after dark."

"Yes, but I need to go back to the palace because of the meeting. I don't want anything like last night to happen again." He would understand the importance of protecting the guests. His father would attend the meeting. Maybe he would be there as well.

"I'm really not sure, though. I'd like to have someone there who has done this before. I can help, but I don't know how good it will be."

"Please, you are all we have." There was no one in Saardam who knew that much about magic, barring Duke Lothar, if he was indeed in Saardam; but if he was, Johanna had seen no sign of him. Or maybe Natalya, but Johanna wasn't sure what she knew or how much to trust her.

CHAPTER 13

LI FAI AGREED to come with her to check out the trees and put wards on them if possible. They left the cabin and its wonderful nutty scent for the fresh morning air.

On the deck, one of Li Han's domestic staff, a middle-aged woman dressed in a dark tunic, stood with a bowl casting handfuls of grain into the duck pen. The birds went head-down in a frenzy, gobbling up as much of the grain as quickly as they could. The woman shouted and waved the bucket when the ducks became too eager. Then she noticed Li Fai and bowed to him, and also to Johanna.

Li Fai helped Johanna down the steep gangplank, where the coach still waited, with Anton and the driver watching without the slightest expressions of puzzlement on their faces.

Johanna told Anton that she wanted to go to the tree in the marketplace.

It was only a short ride from the quay. As Li Fai had rightly noted, stallholders were already arriving with their produce. A bit further down the canal, cheeses were being unloaded from punts and carried up to the market house to be weighed and registered.

The tree that held Alexandre's spirit stood lonely and forlorn. The trunk was twisted, the branches grew stunted and gnarled, and the leaves were marked with ugly white patterns. It was a sickly looking thing that a gardener or farmer would have chopped up for firewood long ago.

Li Fai climbed from the coach first and did Anton's job of helping Johanna down the awkward ladder. A gust of wind blew his jacket and shirt open, showing a bit of his soft-skinned chest. Johanna debated telling him that one of his shirt buttons wasn't done up properly, but she might embarrass him. And maybe, if there was another gust of wind, she might see his skin again.

"That thing makes me very uncomfortable," he said.

"Yes, me, too."

She approached the tree slowly. It was such a weird and twisted thing, with bunches of closely spaced branches growing out of the trunk at random places, with a bark whose grain resembled the patterns made by swirls of ink dropped into water. A couple of people had stopped to look. Johanna had heard only a fraction of the rumours that went around the city about her involvement with the tree: that the tree looked like this because she knitted it together from a couple of brooms, that she used it to spy on everyone and that she could talk to the trapped spirit and it would reply.

She reached out for the trunk, but Li Fai grabbed her arm. "Don't touch it."

"I have to. It is how I can tell if anyone has been here and tried to interfere with the tree."

"I can feel the evil in this tree. Have you touched it before?"

"I have." Not very often, and not since Kylian had come to town. Last time, she had been transported to the previous day, when scores of people walked past getting their daily groceries, ordering supplies for their households, bringing cheeses.

"Did it ever show you a working of the art?"

"No. Not at all. It just shows me the usual things that wood shows me: the things that have happened in this place previously."

He retreated, but the expression on his face showed that he didn't like it.

Johanna touched the tree's trunk and was transported to yesterday afternoon, when the summer evening had turned golden and the stallholders had already closed their businesses and were packing up their wares.

A little boy pulled his mother's hand to get closer to the tree. His mother gave it one look with a horrified expression on her face. "Come. Don't look at that dreadful thing. You'll turn into a ghost if you do."

The boy turned to her and asked in a perfectly serious voice, "What is it like to be a ghost?"

"Don't ask such things!" his mother scolded.

"But I want to know!"

"No one knows, because everyone who becomes a ghost is dead."

The boy frowned. "You mean like grandma?"

"By the Triune, what is wrong with you today? Let's go home straight away."

"I only asked a question!" the boy cried.

"It's been enough of that now. I don't understand why you're always so fascinated by this dreadful thing. We're going home."

The boy kept looking at the tree while his mother dragged him away.

Johanna shivered. That look in his eyes chilled her. She

didn't know the woman or the boy, but there was no doubt that the boy had magic.

"Johanna, Johanna." Li Fai pulled her hand away from the trunk.

Johanna looked at him. "Yes, what's going on?"

"Didn't you hear me at all?"

"What did you say?" She frowned at him.

"I was getting worried about you. Come away from that twisted thing."

"Can you put a ward around it? I don't think anyone has tried to free the spirit yet."

Li Fai pulled a face. He had his hand in his pocket where he probably hid his dragon box. The dragon was a coward, huh? That was not how she had seen it. "It's hard doing it while there are so many people around. I'll come back tonight and try to do it."

Johanna let her gaze roam the marketplace, the quay and the cheese sellers waiting at the weigh house. He was right.

"Come." He drew her away from the tree and led her back to the coach.

"To the palace, Your Majesty?" Anton asked.

"Not yet. I want to check the Shepherd's old house."

He nodded and jumped up on the bench with the driver, while Li Fai helped Johanna up the little ladder.

"I hope I will be able to put up the wards. That tree has bad art," he said, when they sat opposite each other in the coach.

"I know."

"I don't think you know even half of what's going on. The tree puts thoughts into people's minds. It makes people think that it's just an ugly tree—"

"It is an ugly tree."

"Yes, it is, but it's much more."

"It's a prison for an evil spirit. We trapped the tyrant

Alexandre in there. If you cut open the tree, you would find his bones ground to dust."

"There is a lot more than ground bones inside. Can't you see the evil straining against the bark?"

She frowned at him and then looked out the little window as the coach jolted into motion. "Do you see that now?" She had never seen anything of the sort. The trunk was just covered with bark. It was a kind of twisted bark, and she suspected that the wood underneath was also twisted, but there was nothing else remarkable about it. Trees grew like that sometimes. She understood trees.

"I could see it. The trunk glows with evil magic. When you touched it, the glow spread over your hand. I told you to get away from it, but you didn't hear me."

"Well, that's . . ." She frowned at him, disturbed. She didn't remember him having said anything.

"That's why I said not to touch it."

"But I did, and it did no harm to me. I saw nothing remarkable except people from the town going about their normal business." But that little boy had magic. He had known that the tree was special.

There was something she was missing, some clue. Something that Kylian knew and that she would know if only she knew the signs.

"You should go home," Li Fai said. "You don't want to risk yourself and the child by exposing yourself to bad magic."

Johanna laughed. "Most of the bad magic is inside the child. It's why a lot of these things are happening. I want to check out the other tree as well. You can tell me what you see there. If this is Kylian's doing, it's very different from last time he tried to capture the city." *And succeeded.* "He came to the ball and danced with all the girls. Alexandre and his men were hiding in the baron's ships and Kylian disappeared from the palace as soon as the barbarians started setting fire to the houses. This time, I haven't even seen Kylian yet. All the magic is hidden, so that no one suspects anything and there is no reason for anyone to be alert. We don't even know how to organise ourselves to try and fight it."

"You can't fight magic except with magic."

Johanna had heard that before. "I'm afraid, because we're unprepared, I'm alone, and I'm not at my best. I have to take care of the meeting and can't be where I want to go."

"You're not alone. You have me and your daughter."

"But I'm reasonably sure that she is Kylian's."

"She will belong to whomever teaches her first."

"How do you teach infants? They don't listen."

"May I?" Li Fai moved to the bench next to her. He placed his hand on her stomach. A warm glow spread out from the spot where he touched her.

"What is that? How do you do that?"

He withdrew his hand. The glow vanished. "Does it hurt?"

"No, it feels . . . good."

"Every night when you go to bed, put your hands there, and then think about good and happy things. When a child is born with the art, its art is neither good nor evil. It is the men that make it one way or the other. If you train her to have good thoughts then she will more easily understand the value of using her art for good when the time comes to teach. When she is born, stroke her bare head a few times a day. I've heard old midwives say that when the infant is born, the mother must be the first to touch the child's skin, even before it has fully emerged. That way, the child feels that there are others with the art. Those are the things that should be done."

Johanna nodded. She would do them. Soon.

"It surprises me that there are not more people in this town with evil art."

"There was never much magic here. Any people with any ability came from outside, like my mother."

But there were other children with magic in town. They must be taught or the neglect of their ability might well lead to these children becoming disciples of men like Alexandre, which, she suddenly realised, could hold for Octavio Nieland as well. Almost all noble families had links to other towns. The advice about newborn infants must be made known to all the midwives and the mothers. They must find someone wise and experienced to teach older children.

"Thank you," she said softly. "You're helping me a lot."

"I don't know. The work must be done by you. It is not easy or quick, but will be rewarding. It is when the art is neglected that it turns dark and makes people evil."

"Many of us are afraid of magic. Most of us don't know anything about it. Can you teach us?"

"I could, if my father decides to stay. That depends on the negotiations."

"Would he really go to Anglia?"

Li Fai shrugged. He averted his eyes.

"You want to stay, right?"

He nodded, slowly, and let a deep silence lapse. The coach's wheel rattled on the cobblestones. The driver and Anton were laughing.

"I want you to stay, too."

Li Fai met her eyes with an intense look. Johanna's heart was thudding so loud that she could barely hear anything else. He leaned with his elbows on his knees, clasping his hands together so tightly that the knuckles were white.

She lifted her hand, and placed it on top of his.

He shook his head. "Maybe it would be better if we left. This is not right. I . . ." He pulled his hands out from underneath hers. "You have better things to do than worry about me. I am only a merchant's son and I'm—I'm sorry. Forget I said all of this."

He met her eyes, breathing through widened nostrils.

Johanna's cheeks burned. "Li Fai, I—"

The coach came to a halt. Li Fai gasped and jumped back to the bench opposite her, his cheeks bright red.

CHAPTER 14

ANTON WALKED around the coach and opened the door. He helped Johanna down the steps, with Li Fai following close behind. The wind had picked up and the grey clouds released the occasional spitting drops of rain.

"Wow." Li Fai looked up at the house, long since abandoned by the Shepherd and his young family. The tree on the second floor had mangled the house. It had broken through the roof. Its branches spread over the house and part of the neighbours' roofs. Roots as thick as a man's thigh had come out the broken upstairs bedroom window and grown down the façade of the house, between the windows, down the side of the steps to the front door and forced open the door into the servants' entry downstairs.

It was a type of tree Johanna was unfamiliar with and no one had ever seen in Saardam, probably because the box it had grown from was made of foreign wood brought by Li Fai. How the tree survived was anyone's guess, because no one watered it.

"It's grown so much bigger," Li Fai said, his voice low.

"Haven't you been back here since we defeated the relic?"

He shook his head. "This place has bad art. I don't like it."

No, Johanna didn't like it either. Whenever she came past the house, a chill ran over her back, and that same chill now made the hairs on the back of her arms stand up.

Johanna didn't want to go into that house. Evil rolled from it in waves. But if Kylian or someone else had returned and was trying to free the evil from the tree, this would be the place that he did it: the marketplace was much too exposed to too many curious gazes.

Slowly, she climbed the steps to the front door. It stood open, having been wrenched from its frame by fat tree roots. A scent of must and dead leaves wafted from the dark maw. In the months since she and Li Fai had defeated the relic, tree roots had grown across every room, pushing up carpets and floorboards. Animals had moved in.

At some point, the family's servants had been in to remove whatever of the family's furniture had survived the struggle with the relic, but hadn't been back since. It was a sign of the level of evil that reigned here that none of the city's many poor had been in to clear out the items left behind. A table stood, in the middle of what might once have been a sitting room, attached to the floor through thick roots that descended from the ceiling, encasing the table in their stranglehold and disappearing again through the floor.

Johanna clamped her arms around herself. The warmth of summer had not yet penetrated the inside of the house. It was very dark here, despite the fact that it was fully light outside. Mice and rats scurried in the darkness out of her field of vision and from somewhere upstairs came the chirping of little nestling birds.

The last time she had come here, the stairwell had been dark, but tidy, with a dark red runner on the steps and a big clock against the upstairs wall. The runner now lay at the bottom of the stairs. Johanna had to climb over it. The carpet was wet and made squishy sounds under her feet. Rats had chewed holes in the carpet and left their smelly mess in the corners. The clock in the upstairs hallway . . . had sprouted branches.

It was the oddest sight ever. The clock face was stuck at a quarter to twelve, wrenched out of place by sprouting buds. They were oak leaves, because the clock was made from oak wood.

Li Fai stopped to look at it. He rolled one of the leaves between his fingertips. "Interesting."

The clock had grown roots, too, and because the large tree in the spare bedroom—the one that trapped the relic— had shattered the roof, dark stripes from rain water had stained the walls and caused the paint to peel and grow mould.

The upstairs hallway was like a humid, lush cave, with moss-covered tree roots crossing the walls and floor. It reminded her uncomfortably of the ice cellar that she had inadvertently stumbled into when running from the bandits on Duke Lothar's estate.

Johanna hesitated.

Li Fai was at her back—she could feel the warmth of his presence—and though she could never sense magic in the air, the pulse of it was so strong that she could feel *something* there, even if it was not the same sensation as someone with wind magic would feel.

That pulsing sensation wafted out of the door to the spare bedroom.

The room itself was little changed since she had last left it. The tree that grew through the roof had behaved like a normal tree in that its crazy rate of growth had slowed. It was a strange type of tree, unknown to her, with smooth bark and tiny leaves.

The Shepherd's tables and cabinets still stood around the walls, mostly with their macabre contents intact. Daggers, skulls, knives, teeth, beads carved from bone. All these items lay as when she had last come here, albeit now covered in a layer of dust.

The roots of the tree had crushed the box that had contained the relic, and fragments of it lay on the floor, some of them having sprouted branches and roots of their own. It was like an eerie dark forest in here.

She took a deep breath and reached out for the trunk of the tree. Li Fai wanted to stop her, but she insisted, "I have to do this."

As soon as a hands touched the smooth tree bark, her vision faded.

The anger of the magic pulsed within the wood. It was much clearer than the magic in the tree in the market place.

The relic was trapped, not defeated.

A vision now came to her. It was dark in the room and someone was coming closer with a storm light that bobbed up and down with the bearer's footsteps. A pale face glowed in the candlelight, and another one. Two boys snuck in from the hallway. The one carrying the storm light put it down on one of the cabinets. He looked around the room.

"Oh, wow, you are right, this is so amazing!"

"Don't touch anything, though. Some of these things are bewitched." The second boy wore a coat that was far too big for him and a cap that shaded his face. He carried a box under his arm that he set on the floor and removed the lid from. On a bed of cloth that looked like it had been cut from an old curtain lay an assortment of the kind of things boys typically collected from the shores of the river and the beach: empty mussel shells, bird skulls, dried sea weed, bits of gnarled wood and polished rocks.

"I want that one," the first boy said, still looking at the

cabinets in the room. He pointed at a dagger that lay by itself in a glass cabinet. It was an old, dirty and crooked thing, and had a dark heft with inlaid silver and a stained blade. The only thing that looked clean was the ruby set at the pommel.

"No, you can't. That's an evil thing."

"You're just saying that so you can have it."

"If I wanted to have it, wouldn't I already have taken it before bringing you here?"

The boy turned to his friend, comprehension dawning on his face. "But . . . how do you know that it's evil?"

"The heft is made of silver and bone. The jewel in the top is a ruby. Those are the things that magicians use."

"You know you scare me sometimes? How do you know all these things?"

The other boy didn't answer that question. He had picked up a little glass jar and rolled the contents—some kind of seeds—around by the light of the lamp.

Johanna recognised him as the boy who had wanted to go to the tree in the market place. The boy with magic. He studied the seeds in the same chilling, calculating way that the tone of his voice had displayed. Too mature for his age.

"What are you doing?" the other boy wanted to know.

The magic boy unstoppered the jar and shook out some of the seeds into the palm of his hand.

"They're just seeds," his friend said, but his voice sounded dubious. "What are you going to do with those?"

The magic boy let the seeds drop on the ground. "If you were a tree, how would you feel about growing all alone on the top floor of a house?"

"Well, I . . ." His friend gave the magic boy a strange look. "That's rubbish, Rue. Trees don't feel, at least not like people do."

"How do you know that?" He put the jar back into his pocket and studied the cabinets. "This is a thing that you can have." He opened one of the glass doors and took a dusty piece of pottery from the shelf, a little statue of a naked troll.

His friend was still fascinated by the dagger with the ruby on top. The magic boy collected a few other things: a roll of parchment, a handful of old silver coins, and a skull of a bird with a long crooked beak.

He put these in the box with the rest of his collection, pointing out how each of these things was special. Then he said, "Will you stop looking at that dagger!"

"But I want it," the other boy said.

"You can't have it. Come, that thing is going to bewitch you. I shouldn't have brought you here." He put the lid back on the box.

"And so you were going to keep all this for yourself?"

"Will you stop it? This is the Shepherd's house. It's not yours, and it's not mine either."

He more or less pushed the other boy out of the room.

When they were gone, a faint glow lit up on the floor, as the seeds that the boy had dropped sprouted and grew little plants. And then nothing more happened, because there were no more visions.

Johanna shivered.

She remembered Li Fai saying *It is when the art is neglected that it turns dark and makes people evil.*

"What did you see?" Li Fai asked behind her.

"The only people who have been in here were two boys collecting bits of curiosa. One of them has magic, but he's far too young to have anything to do with Kylian."

Still, something about the vision didn't sit well with her. Why had he thrown out the seeds? Who was this boy?

She clamped her arms around herself.

Li Fai studied the cabinets around the room, bending over in the semidarkness to look at this or that object, but not touching anything.

She touched his arm, disturbed by how warm he felt and how very cold she felt. "Come on, let's go. This place scares me."

"It is not a comfortable place." He continued looking at the objects on the shelf, squinting in the low light.

"What are you doing?" she asked.

"I'm not sure. Something in here still feels . . . alive."

"The dagger," she said, before she could stop herself.

He let his gaze roam over the shelves. "Which dagger?"

"The one with the—" The spot where it had lain in her vision was empty. That was . . . odd. The vision had not shown her that anyone else had been in here after the boys left. She told Li Fai about what she had seen. He knelt on the ground where the boy had dropped the seeds. Only a few desiccated stalks remained, which he picked up and held on the outstretched palm of his hand. "Do you recognise this plant?"

"From just those stalks? It seems like some sort of garden weed to me. Give them. I might ask Roald."

He handed the stalks to her, and she opened the little powder box in her purse and dropped them in.

"The art is even stronger in this house," Li Fai said. "If I wanted to lay a ward, I could perhaps do it for the tree in the markets, at night when no one is watching. I'd have no chance with this construct of evil. It would require a capable master."

"You're more capable than you think. I've seen your dragon."

"It's nice of you to say so, but no, I don't believe that."

A short silence followed his words, in which Johanna's frustration at her own inability to fully comprehend magic boiled over. In fact, did *anyone* understand it?

"We better go now anyway," Johanna said. "Or I'll be late for the meeting."

"Yes. I was going to go to the palace with my father. I better make sure he doesn't spend too much time worrying about where I am."

They went outside into the light and the gentle warmth of a cloudy summer morning in Saardam.

The coach was waiting and Anton stood on the steps of the house. The relief on his face when he saw her was disturbing. "Oh, Your Majesty, there you are. I was getting worried, because we need to go back to the palace—"

"I know. We can return home now."

Anton held open the door for her and helped her in. "Quick, Your Majesty. We are going to be quite late already."

Johanna looked around, but Li Fai wasn't following her into the coach.

He said, "I can walk from here. You go home quickly before your father gets worried."

Johanna nodded. Father *would* be worried.

She waved to Li Fai. Anton shut the door and jumped up on the driver's seat. The coach jolted and then Li Fai was gone from view, and Johanna was left alone with her worries. She had two tasks: she should bring the negotiations to a success and she should stop Kylian or his minions from reviving the evil relic or Alexandre's spirit.

There might not be time to do both of them properly. There might not even be time to complete one of the tasks within the short time she had.

AT THE PALACE Johanna found most of the men already at the table, surprised that she was late. She crossed the room in quick strides and sat down to polite nods. A young girl came to bring her breakfast.

There were cheeses and bread and jams and cooked eggs, everything the foreign guests might want. Johanna ate as much as she could, which wasn't much these days. She knew that she'd be hungry later.

For the number of people at the table, the gathering was surprisingly quiet. Duke Aroden sat bent over, staring at his plate. The duchess glanced at Johanna a dark expression on her face. Earl Maximilian was not eating at all. Baron Uti was eating, but doing so quietly. His face and bald head shone with sweat. Ignatius Hemeldinck and Fleuris LaFontaine sat by his side, both pale-faced.

Only King William was being his loud self, but several of the members of King Benito's party cast him dagger looks across the table. King Benito himself sat scowling at his plate.

Roald had not yet turned up. She should go and check on him if she had a little time, but it was probably just as well if he didn't come on the trip, with all potential for disasters that would entail.

Father had come to breakfast with all his notes and papers, and as soon as the servants started to clear away the plates, he folded out his plans and explained what they would do for the rest of the day. More than a few of the guests looked unimpressed.

Johanna glanced at King William, who looked pretty pleased with himself. Just what was his game? Making sure this meeting didn't succeed?

To be honest, she couldn't muster much enthusiasm for leading an excursion into the fields and all over town. She could have easily gone to bed and slept all day. And she hadn't even attended the drinking party.

Father and Master Deim had devised a very full program. First they would look at all the warehouses in the harbour, and then they would cross the little creek outside the city to have a look at the farms that would have to be cleared in order for new warehouses to be built. One of the guests asked what they would do for lunch. Father informed him that a few people from farms were going to bring food to an old farmhouse shed that was empty but in a good enough condition to stop for the midday meal and be dry if it rained.

Then breakfast was done and everyone went to dress for their expedition.

Johanna saw Nellie in the dressing room. After the initial gloominess, the day promised to become sunny again and most of her dresses were quite warm.

"I hate it how I spend all my days feeling hot," Johanna said.

"It will soon be over," Nellie said. She put Johanna's hair up in a bun and pinned down the stray strands.

Johanna was already sweating. It was so incredibly tempting to claim sickness.

Before leaving the room, she looked at herself in the mirror. "I look like a fat cow. An overcooked fat cow. How can anyone take me seriously?"

"I don't think you do. You look very pretty and motherly."

That was just the problem. Why had she ever thought this was a good idea? She had enough of being like this. She didn't care how much it hurt and what people would say. She wanted the child out.

Johanna met Father and all the other guests in the foyer. This time, local businessmen had also turned up, including Li Han with Li Fai, who met her eyes with an intense look. The harbour master had come with a couple of merchants, including, she noticed with dread, Octavio Nieland, who stood talking to Fleuris LaFontaine and Ignatius Hemeldinck. When his cold gaze met hers, he stuck his chin up. Johanna turned away from him, but could still feel his stare prick her neck.

Father led the group outside.

Smartly dressed guards and coachmen waited at the doors, ready to take the guests to their coaches.

Johanna's coach with the white horses stood in front. Johanna rode alone this time, because it would simply not do to show preference to one of the guests over the others.

The caravan set off through the palace gates. People in the street stopped to watch the spectacle of coaches and horses and dapper-looking coachmen. They cheered and waved to Johanna. She sat stiffly in front of the little window in the coach's door to wave back. Her attention was drawn to a man with a little girl at a street corner. Years ago, that might have been her. When that girl was older, she might say, "Do you remember the time that all the kings came to town?" And it would be a defining moment that everyone remembered.

She, ordinary Johanna Brouwer, of merchant, not noble, descent, would have to make sure there would be something else to add to the memories of those people, so they would say, "Yes, dear, that was when the agreement was signed and we've never had a war since."

So much hinged on these few days that she could not allow herself to be distracted. Even magic would have to be dealt with later.

The first stop was the harbour. The coaches stopped in front of the ruined ammunitions depot and the party gathered at the point where the eastern arm split off from the main quay. From this position, you could see King William's ship side-on. It towered over the other ships in the harbour.

The focus of this stop was the ruined ammunitions depot.

Father explained that the harbourmaster had applied to have it moved out of this position, so that the site would come free for development. He suggested that offices and warehouses should be built for the biggest investors.

"Mooring space is going to be a problem here," King Leopold said.

To this, Father explained that there was a canal along the back, and that the plan was to widen it. Here, the harbourmaster took over and detailed some of the necessary buildings. He hinted at the fact that Saardam might be a future base for iron ships, which needed fuel, and that needed to be stored somewhere; and the making of those ships would require more and bigger halls.

"I'm guessing all this is just a way of softening us up for a doubling of mooring fees?" King William stood with his hands behind his back.

Oh, the terrible boor. Was he always like this? Johanna said, "No one who cannot afford the fees and who has helped invest in these developments will pay any."

The men turned around and stared at her. King William let out a bellow of a laugh that echoed over the harbour.

"Would you mind keeping it down a little?" Duke Aroden asked.

It was time to go to the next stop. Johanna dragged herself to the coach. All of a sudden, she was so incredibly tired. She met Li Fai's eyes while Anton helped her up the ladder. He waited next to his father to board one of the other coaches. He acted very proper: not a nod, not a smile. But he had been looking at her a lot today, and she wondered about what he had been trying to tell her this morning in the coach to the Shepherd's house, and she wondered what would have happened had the coach not stopped at that moment.

It was not right, he'd said.

Of course she knew what wasn't right, or at least she thought she did. Or she *hoped.*

It could only mean that he felt for her in the same way she felt for him, right? That a glimpse of soft skin sent her heart racing, that his smile made her cheeks glow.

The coach started moving with a jolt, but went at a slow pace to allow the others to keep up. Johanna squinted into the bright sunlight, struggling to keep her eyes open.

The next stop was East Harbour, where the fire damage had been limited to a few spot fires. Several of the warehouses were empty here, because the owners had moved elsewhere after the fires. Only the very far end of the harbour was deep enough for seafaring vessels, and this was where the Nieland family's *Josephine* lay. The ship had sustained some damage when a neighbouring ship on fire—rumour went that it had been the *Lady Davida*—had bumped into the hull and made deep scorch marks on the otherwise pristine vessel.

As to why, a year after the fires, the damaged ship had still not been fixed, well, people said that the ship builders had refused to deal with the Nieland family because of Octavio's support for Alexandre. It was a wonder that he hadn't left town yet, but additional rumours said that he would leave immediately once his father died.

Nothing escaped King William's sharp gaze. "Why has no one put that worm-ridden old barge over there out of its misery? Was it so bad that not even the bandits wanted it?"

Several men—visitors and clueless ones—laughed.

Octavio hissed. "What makes *you* think that you can come here and insult us?"

King William laughed again. "Boy, they do have feisty merchants in this place."

Octavio rushed forward. Johanna saw what was happening and managed to step into his path. He almost crashed into her. "Get out of my way, woman." Spit flew from his mouth.

She put her hands on her hips.

Master Deim joined her. He stared at Octavio. Octavio glared back.

"Learn to control your temper, man," Master Deim said, his voice low.

"Did you hear what he said?"

"He's here to provoke, and succeeding admirably. Ignore him."

"When you're courting him to *buy land* in *our* town?"

"Buying the rights to use warehouse space," Johanna corrected.

"And whose stupid idea was that?" His gaze bored into hers. "By the holy god, stupid woman, do you even know what you're playing with?"

"Yes," Johanna said. "Grown men who behave like toddlers."

His nostrils flared. His muscles in his shoulders strained. For a moment, she was afraid that he would hit her, but he came to his senses, stuck his chin in the air and turned around.

King William laughed again. By the Triune, that man was annoying.

"That's not a good enemy to have," Master Deim said to Johanna in a low voice.

"He was never going to be a proponent," Johanna said. "Better that we know where he stands in the open so that everyone else can see it, too." But she was trembling and sweating in her hot dress.

Father continued with his presentation unperturbed.

Even if Octavio Nieland was not interested, King Leopold seemed to warm to the idea of having dedicated warehouse space. He asked about prices and how taxes and harbour fees would be handled. Father and Master Deim dealt with his questions.

King Benito looked on with a scowl, but she understood that this was a normal expression for him. He asked a few questions, most of them practical, which indicated to Johanna that he was interested, too. Seeing that, King William couldn't afford to stay behind, and he out-questioned everyone else, except Johanna wasn't sure that he was completely serious.

Towards midday, the caravan of coaches left the city through the old gates. The fields were lush and green and full of flowers, cows grazed and the scene would have been utterly peaceful if it weren't for the burnt-out shell of the farmhouse that stood on a hillock surrounded by willow trees. A shed a bit further down appeared to have survived the fires. The coaches stopped at the creek crossing, where a couple of young men waited to punt them across the sluggishly flowing water.

From there, the party waded through the thigh-high grass the short distance to the burnt-out house up the riverbank. Two carthorses stood in the yard, tied to a tree. The farm cart waited in the shelter of the barn, which had both doors open.

A farmer and a woman young enough to be his daughter sat in the driver's seat. The flat tray on the cart, scrubbed to within and inch of its life, bore a selection of serving trays, each with plates of local produce. There was roast duck, chicken and pork, pickled mussels, cheeses, pâtés, smoked sausages and plenty of fresh bread. The farmer's daughter handed out plates, and a woman who was probably the girl's mother brought cider, and water for finger bowls.

The cider, especially, met with a lot of approval.

Once everyone had a plate, the group dispersed around the barn.

Johanna's feet ached, and she had to sit down on the dusty haystack in the corner of the barn. Many of the men remained standing. She ended up close to a group that contained Li Han, his son and a couple of Estlander merchants. Li Han appeared to know these men, judging by the way they were laughing and talking. Johanna would look at Li Fai, at the way he moved his hands when he spoke, and how utterly serious his face looked. He glanced in between his father's acquaintances a few times, meeting her eyes squarely.

She then averted her gaze, studying the walls and ceiling instead, while her heart thudded audibly and her cheeks glowed.

This farm had lain abandoned for quite a while and the barn was full of cobwebs. The farming family had left long before the fires. The land belonged to one of the noble families and they had never been more than caretakers. This area had a tendency to flood and, after losing all their cattle in a flood, the family was forced to set up elsewhere. Alexandre's bandits had set fire to the house last year.

The walls still stood, but the roof had fallen in. The scent of burned wood was gone, and weeds grew in the corners of the house's rooms. The overgrown yard was surrounded by willow trees, and the land sloped down to the river shore and marshy ground where a riot of plants flowered.

This area was the masterpiece of Father and Master Deim's plans and when most of the men had eaten their fill, Father started his talk.

Master Deim hung up the map on the inside of the farm door and explained how they would build a wall around the tongue of land, and how they would use windmills to makes sure the land remained dry. He gave all his calculations of how many stones would be needed to build seawalls, how much sand would have to be carried in to make the ground safe from flooding in the future, and where bridges would be built to connect the area to the rest of the city without the need for a punt. Also, the creek would have to be dug out so that bigger vessels could come in, not to speak of the warehouses and shipyards that would be built once all those things had been done.

The men were now definitely intrigued.

"Turn this useless piece of land into market space?" Baron Uti scoffed. "Why not use another piece of land?"

But some of the others were asking questions about the techniques. The idea of pumping water out with windmills was nothing new, just the thought of applying it over such a big area.

Master Deim answered all the questions without once mentioning the name of Rinius, who was the originator of many of the ideas.

Even King William appeared intrigued. At the very least, he had stopped laughing. His face bore a small frown, and occasionally he would speak to the earl in a low voice. Johanna understood that flooding could be a problem in parts of the Anglian capital, Targon, as well.

Johanna had heard about the ideas so often the she knew them by heart, and she trusted Father and Master Deim to deliver the ideas in a way that businessmen understood. That seemed to be her lot: stay in the background and let the men carry out her plans. A sad thing, but it was the only way the kings would accept it.

She studied the faces of the guests. King William appeared intrigued. The man was annoyingly awake after that late night. Some of the other men were yawning and looked as wilted as she felt. Duke Aroden's face was positively grey. She had already spotted him dashing off into the bushes twice.

Li Han and his son were also unusually bright and alert, not having attended the party last night, and the early morning trip didn't seem to have affected Li Fai in the slightest. She understood he usually rose very early.

Johanna picked bits of hay out of her dress. Nellie would probably complain about getting dust and sticks on her clothes, but she didn't care. Hopefully, soon after all these men left, she would be able to put this dress in the wardrobe and never touch it again.

Unless she had another child. Roald's this time, although she doubted that would be possible.

The farmer's daughter brought another round of cider. The men made toasts. Some of them were getting entirely too cheerful again. Duke Aroden was arguing, red-cheeked, with Ignatius Hemeldinck. He slurred his words and his movements were jerky. Johanna felt sorry for Duchess Carlotta.

More cider was served. This time, even Father and Master Deim were drinking, although not nearly as much as some of the others.

Then Baron Uti asked in a loud voice, "These building plans are all very well, but there is the remaining issue with the Church. I'm afraid that most of us would be unwilling to condone investment in this city when it is ruled by a church that forbids *our* church and that actively campaigns against our morals."

Father said, "Saardam is not ruled by the church. We also have a Belaman Church for those who wish to attend it. Most of the nobles do, in fact."

"But the king comes from a strong background of support for the Church of the Triune."

Now Johanna felt pressured to speak up. "The king is not his father. We—the king, myself and the King's Council—see the problems caused by King Nicholaos and his over-generous donations to the church."

The Baron blinked, as if he wanted to say, *What's that woman doing here?* "Where does the king stand in this matter?" His cheeks were red from the cider.

"The king is well-educated in various branches of the church. You will know that he spent some time at the farm of the Guentherite brotherhood—"

King William sucked in a breath. "Are those bandits still around?"

"Watch it," King Leopold said. "They are honest, law-abiding citizens. A religious order. It's ludicrous to use the word bandits for them. Bandits are the rogues that live in the woods and make passage of the rivers hazardous."

Baron Uti protested. "Hey, what are you looking at me for?"

"It's your brother who's doing that."

"I have no brother." The Baron tightened his arms over his chest.

Johanna stepped in. "Gentlemen, I can assure you that the Church of the Triune will have nothing to do with this project, at least not in any way that limits your business concerns."

Baron Uti glared at her.

Then someone else said, "Well, I don't really want to spoil

the pretty queen's party but that silly church has a pretty good grip on this town these days."

Johanna looked in the direction of the voice. It was Octavio Nieland. He gave her a hard, emotionless look.

"I agree," Fleuris LaFontaine said. "That church has got its tendrils everywhere."

Johanna glared at him. *And the Belaman Church doesn't? They even try to control us from Seneza.* "I assure everyone that the Church of the Triune will *not* interfere with any of your businesses or any of the people you bring into our city. I cannot see any representatives of the church here and they will not sign any of the agreements. They are not involved."

An uncomfortable silence followed her words. Then the farmer's daughter came in again with another barrel of cider, and some of the men cheered.

Johanna couldn't bear the tension anymore. These men were going to get horribly drunk yet again, and they were going to come to fisticuffs soon. And she did not want to be present when that happened.

She got up and left the barn. Father looked at her, but didn't say anything. Li Fai looked at her, too, but didn't say anything either.

The fatigue and aching overwhelmed her. She felt powerless, she wanted to go home and sleep, she couldn't do this anymore.

The overgrown garden blurred before her eyes.

This had been a bad idea. These men had come here only to hold drinking parties, and to fight with each other. Her project never had a chance. They had come here to steal her ideas, and then use them to lure Li Han to *their* towns. And then she would lose Li Fai, and all his knowledge about magic.

She would lose what had never been hers.

CHAPTER 16

JOHANNA PUSHED through the tall grass. She had to get out of here, had to go somewhere to compose herself, to gather her frayed nerves and push away that all-pervading feeling that she had failed at everything she had attempted. They didn't need her at the meeting, she wasn't wanted there and most of the kings and dukes didn't take her seriously. It was *her* idea, and now Father and Master Deim were taking all the credit and answering all the questions.

But at least it was happening. She shouldn't behave like a child. Life wasn't fair, especially if you were a commoner woman.

She reached the water's edge and continued along the riverbank. The grass was tall here, and full of buttercups and caraway. A couple of coots skittered from the reeds that lined the river and flew low over the water. Roald would love it here.

"Johanna."

She turned around. It was Li Fai. Something in her had known that it would be him. She had seen this situation in her vision. Possible futures he'd said, and now she understood. She had a choice. She could lead him back to the barn where the men were drinking and arguing, or she could walk with him . . . until the next choice presented itself.

He caught up with her, wading through the long grass, and she led him up the little rise. From the other side, you could look over the wide expanse of the Saar delta. Saardam lay to the left: rows of brightly painted houses that looked a bit strange without the tower of the main church. None of the sounds from the city penetrated here. In fact, the only sounds were the soft lapping of the water against the shore, the sighing of the summer breeze through the weeping willow branches and the warbling of a lark overhead.

Johanna picked her way through the long grass to the little beach at the end. A tree trunk lay half on the sand, half in the water. Johanna sat down on it. She undid the restricting buckles to her shoes, slipped her feet out and stuck them in the water. It was lovely and cool. A few tadpoles skittered out of the way.

Li Fai sat down next to her, without saying a word. He pulled an apple from his pocket, put both his thumbs next to the stem and pulled it apart, neatly splitting the apple in half. He held one half out to her.

Johanna shook her head. "I'm sorry, but apples give me a terrible heartburn."

He bit into the flesh with a great crunch.

"I hate it when they drink so much," Johanna said. "They don't listen, they talk about all these stupid things, like parties they've attended. I feel like I've wasted my time." The river blurred in front of her eyes. She fought away the tears.

"Men are not good when they have been drinking. They say things they would never say otherwise."

They *did* things they would never do otherwise, too, like fight; and if a bunch of kings came to blows over some trivial issue because they seemed to *want* to fight, she would be blamed.

This meeting was going to be a disaster.

She angrily wiped her eyes with the back of her hand. She didn't want to cry. It was so annoying that she tended to burst out into tears with every little thing. Helena had told her that this was common for women with child.

Li Fai was quiet, looking at the water.

"So, what does your father think?" she asked, breaking the uneasy silence. Her voice felt choked.

"He keeps asking me why we should stay when so many people in town keep committing crimes in our name. He says none of our hosts have addressed that."

That was true. She'd had no time to look into the weapons smuggling issue, beyond going to the warehouses and not finding anything of note. Having been too busy guarding the important guests, the guards didn't appear to have made any progress either.

"My father has been talking to King William." There was sadness in his eyes.

Johanna's heart jumped. "You don't want to go to Anglia."

He shook his head. "It is a bleak place where the streets are shrouded in mist half the time and it rains the other half. Everything is grey. There are no people from anywhere else except Anglia and they don't understand different habits. As soon as people see you're from another land, they try to raise their prices so they can make more money from you. It is very hard to know who to trust enough to call a friend. I really don't like that place."

"Do any people there have magic?"

"Not that I've seen, but my father wouldn't care. He doesn't have the art."

"But you could tell him that we would like you to teach and that if you stay, you could have a school of magic. I know there are children in town with magic. They must be taught. *I* could use your teaching."

She met his eyes.

Johanna's heart was thudding. This was the part she had seen in her vision, where . . .

"You do need teaching. Wood art is a special thing. It is powerful and dangerous. There is much to learn about it."

Clearly, he was the best person to do that.

"I'm trying to get your father to stay with our plan, but I don't think it's working. *I* want you to stay. I think we could both greatly benefit from cooperation." She slipped into more formal wording than she wanted. She so desperately wanted this *not* to be about business, and even after all this, she still feared he misunderstood her, and she was afraid to be hurt because of it.

He nodded. And then he whispered, "On the other hand, it could be that you give me a reason to stay."

Johanna met his eyes, seeing herself reflected in his perfectly black irises. This was the part where she made a choice and her life took another turn. She could be proper and lose him, or she could find some happiness.

She didn't know what to do. Even if kings and queens had lovers, the thought made her uncomfortable. Roald was a nice man, in his own way, and she hated to betray him. He needed care and someone to guide him. Being married to him hadn't, overall, turned out as badly as she'd thought.

But did all that mean that she couldn't ever find someone who made her heart beat faster?

The riverbank, reeds and the churning water blurred before her eyes. She blinked hard, but a tear ran across her cheek anyway.

A hand moved into the field of her vision and wiped it off. "You're a strong-willed woman. You can make anything work. Crying doesn't suit you."

"I know," Johanna sobbed. The tears were unstoppable. "I'm just so . . . tired, and I feel stupid—"

"You're not stupid."

"And I feel irrelevant."

"Those men will only be important until they realise that those who matter in today's world, are those with money *and* a wish to make the future better."

"But they pretend I don't exist." Johanna wiped at her face.

"Don't." He held her hand. "You'll smear dirt all over yourself."

"It's powder, not dirt."

"It doesn't look good." He bent down and scooped some water up into his hands. "May I?"

She leaned back and he splashed cool water over her face. The touch of his fingertips was a very pleasant sensation. She lifted her chin.

He massaged her shoulders and the sides of her neck, which were very tense. She wriggled behind her back for the laces of her bodice and pulled them loose, draping the dress' top loosely over her shoulders. He massaged the top of her arms and her back, her skin pale in the sunlight.

She closed her eyes, but peeped between her eyelashes at his oh so serious face while he did this.

He took off his vest, and when he bent over her at a particular angle, she could see right into his shirt. He had no hair on his chest at all. He had none on his chin either.

His face was so close now that she could feel his breath on her skin. His hands had gone from making firm movements to a soft caress. He bent over her shoulder and traced the outline of her shoulder with his lips.

Johanna gasped.

"It upsets you? I'm sorry, I won't do it anymore. I won't—"

"Be quiet and use your tongue for something else."

His eyes widened. He smiled, and then he closed the gap between them and kissed her.

His mouth was soft and tasted of foreign spices. For a long time they sat there, lost in the moment. She leaned into him, replying to his kiss. His hands stroked her shoulders and back and pulled her dress further off her shoulders.

She was going to protest that the others might come, but they were all drunk in the barn, and wouldn't lower themselves by going for a stroll along the river. They would be asleep, badly hung over from the previous day. And she could see or hear them coming from a good distance anyway.

She lowered herself to the sand next to the washed-up tree trunk. When she touched the wood, it showed her that a couple of ducks often slept here, their beaks tucked under their wings.

She pulled her dress over her head. The sunlight was extremely bright on her underdress. It felt warm on her swollen breasts and her round stomach. Li Fai stroked the stretched skin, which was redder and more blotchy than it had ever been.

"That's from being hot all the time. I'm ugly. I look like something bloated and dead."

"You're beautiful." He slid his hand up to her breasts, bunching the dress up.

His touch made her shiver. Her breasts perked up, the nipples dark and firm. He took one in his mouth and rolled it with his tongue. Johanna let her head hang back, breathing deeply. She wanted him so badly. No harm could be done now. To be frank she didn't even care if anyone saw them. Her body screamed out for him.

He teased her, inserting his fingers in the wetness between her legs. With all the pressure of the child in that area, she was so sensitive there.

"Please, do it," she whispered. "Before someone comes. Please."

He loosened his belt and pulled down the front of his trousers. Oh my, he was ready. She reached up and pulled him closer.

"Isn't it going to hurt you?"

"I'll tell you if it does." She wasn't sure that she cared anymore anyway. Could it possibly hurt any more than everything hurt already?

She rolled on her side and pulled the back of her underdress up. "Quick. Do it."

He didn't need telling twice.

CHAPTER 17

WHEN IT WAS DONE, she dozed in his arms. Happy, tired, satisfied. For a moment, she didn't want to think about the implications of what she had just done, and of all the other difficulties facing her.

She could have lain there forever, but the sun was sinking alarmingly, and the others would wonder where she was and would even come looking for her.

So she eased herself from his arms. He smiled at her, and that smile made her heart weep. She pulled down her underdress. The overdress, that horrible stiff thing made by mistress Dina, still lay draped over the tree trunk. She pulled it over her head. Li Fai helped her do up the laces at the back while she tried to brush all the sticks off the skirt.

She jammed her swollen feet back into her shoes. Slowly, they made their way back towards the barn. Butterflies fluttered low over the grass, stopping occasionally to sit on flowers. Bees buzzed and a family of quails ran squawking into a thicket.

It was so beautiful and so warm. She wanted to hold Li

Fai's hand, but didn't dare do so. There would be plenty of talk already.

Her judgement that the men were all asleep turned out to have been right. By the time they entered the farmyard and came back to the barn, King Leopold and Baron Uti were just coming outside, stretching and rubbing their eyes.

King Leopold exclaimed, "Oh! There you are."

"I went for a walk by the river while you were sleeping."

The Baron laughed, but was looking at Li Fai, one eyebrow raised.

Johanna broke the uneasy silence. "We should go back now. The evening meal will be served in the hall."

The barn doors opened and more people came out. King William, with straw in his hair, Earl Maximilian, looking slightly rumpled.

Father and Master Deim sat in the corner in deep discussion with two Anglian merchants. Johanna gathered that they were talking about the building of ships. Were they talking about having the *Lady Davida* rebuilt in Anglia?

Father met Johanna's eyes. She hoped she didn't blush, because Father always had a pretty good idea of what she had been up to.

Li Fai joined his father, who had also taken the opportunity to have a nap.

Walking back to the creek where the punt waited, the group was a lot more subdued than on the way here. Most of the men were quietly talking. The snatches of conversations that she caught indicated friendly discussions, reminiscences and tall tales. The group had sorted into people who got on with each other and hopefully this might mean that there would be no more fights, at least not until the negotiations started tomorrow morning.

Maybe she could get a decent night's sleep tonight.

Li Fai's face was a bit sunburnt. She suspected hers was, as well. Thinking about him still made her glow.

At the other side of the creek, the coaches still waited. Anton helped her into hers. Through the little windows she could see Li Fai and his father climbing into another coach. She remembered the soft feel of his skin. She remembered his hands at her sides. She remembered how he laughed when she found her pleasure, and then went and did it again. Pleasure was meant to be like that. It wasn't just a thing for the man. It was meant to be enjoyed by both.

If his father decided to stay in Saardam, and if she could negotiate a good enough deal so that this was an attractive proposition, and Li Fai taught her magic, he could give her a lesson in the art of loving, too.

By the time they came back to the palace, the long shadows of the poplar trees were creeping over the forecourt. The row of coaches stopped, the order reversed ,from when they had left, with Johanna coming last, so that she didn't have to wait.

As soon as Anton had helped her out, a guard came to talk to him. He nodded, his face serious, and then came to Johanna.

"What is going on?" Johanna asked.

"He says they found more of those smuggled weapons, Your Majesty."

Johanna's heart jumped.

Father was waiting to guide her up the stairs, but she gestured for him to continue.

He protested. "But what about the evening meal?"

"I'll be along later. Go ahead, keep position for me." She wasn't hungry anyway. For the last few days, she'd had a feeling that everything she ate or drank got stuck inside her and refused to come out.

Father did as she said, and she watched him go slowly up the stairs with the group.

"Where did you find them?" she asked Anton in a low voice when the last of the guests were out of earshot.

"In an office that belongs to the Hemeldinck family."

Johanna knew the place. Ignatius' brother owned an accounting firm there.

"Did you arrest anyone in conjunction with it?"

"No. We are following them from a distance to see what they will do now. There seems to be a group of men involved selling weapons in Florisheim."

Master Deim had said that he suspected as much.

"Where are these weapons now?"

"They're in the harbourmaster's office."

"Can you possibly bring them here so I can have a look?"

He bowed. "I can do that, Your Majesty."

He retreated and Johanna continued further up the stairs. By the Triune, she did not want to deal with this now as well as everything else. She went briefly to her private quarters to get changed. At least Roald had managed to get out of bed; that was something.

She met Nellie in the dressing room.

"Oh, goodness, mistress Johanna, your face is sunburnt."

Johanna looked in the mirror. Nellie was right: her cheeks glowed and felt hot. It had been such a long time ago that she had spent any amount of time outside. She stood in front of the mirror for Nellie to help her out of the dress.

"Whatever have you done while you were there?"

"What do you mean?"

"The laces are all tangled up."

"I loosened the dress because it was too tight. And then I couldn't see to do them back up." Her cheeks burned.

Nellie helped her get changed, did her hair. Johanna sat patiently through her ministrations when her attention fell on the powder boxes on the dressing table. By the Triune, she still had the stalks of that plant that had grown in the Shepherd's house in the powder box in her purse. She should show them to Roald to ask him if he knew what sort of plant it was.

When Nellie had finished, she found the box and went into the library.

Roald sat in his usual chair with his nose in a book. Johanna stopped at the door, suddenly overwhelmed by the terrible act of betrayal that she had committed in her very selfish needs.

He didn't notice her, but kept reading, sliding his finger over the page and moving his lips.

Johanna crossed the room, feeling heavy. Should she confess? Would he understand? Would he get angry or start banging his head against the wall?

He lives in his own world. I can look after him, but he won't ever satisfy me in that way. The coming together of a man and a woman required two people to act.

"The evening meal is ready," she said. Her voice sounded high to her ears.

Now he looked up as if it were the first time he had noticed her. He said nothing about her burnt face.

She opened the powder box and carefully extracted the stalk that Li Fai had picked up. "Do you know which plant this is?"

He took the stalk from her and rolled it between his fingers.

Then he sniffed it and studied the leaf fragments that had broken off and that lay in the bottom of that box.

Then he said, "Forget-me-nots."

Johanna knew the pretty blue flowers that often grew in damp pieces of land. "What is the point of forget-me-nots?"

"Don't you know? You give them to a girl you like, and

then the girl forgets everything except you. The forget-me-nots make you forget things."

"Forget. . . ?" She could still see the boy dropping the seeds on the ground in the Shepherd's spare bedroom. He had to have done that on purpose or by order of someone else. And what would have been the reason for him to have dropped the seeds if it wasn't to steal the dagger with the bone and silver hilt and the ruby in the pommel?

What was the relevance? Who was that boy? He did *not* look like an innocent child. He was a child with magic who knew exactly what he was doing. A boy with magic, desperately in need of magical schooling or he would become a miniature version of . . . his father? Was this another one of Kylian's children?

Johanna felt sick. She thought of Li Fai's words about "children with the art". It was a sad thing that when children were born that weren't entirely normal, people would shun them, and even the parents would hide them and attempt to erase them from their lives, like Roald's parents had done to him.

He was still sitting there looking up at her, dependent on her like a child. The room blurred before her eyes. She dropped to her knees in front of him, eased the book out of his hands and enclosed him in a hug. He made a surprised noise.

"Roald, whatever happens, I will look out for you. I will be there to assist you. I may have . . . other needs sometimes, but that doesn't mean that I love you less. You're my family, my brother."

He said nothing for a long time, as he was wont to do in situations like this, and then he said, "Does this mean that you want me to do something like go to dinner?"

"No. You can do what you want."

"Good, because my head hurts and I don't want to go to

dinner. Those men only want me there so that they can laugh at me."

"I know. They laugh at me, too. But they won't be laughing much longer."

Johanna really needed to go to the dining hall, so she wrestled herself to her feet—it was disturbing how hard that was when you were as heavy and unbalanced as she was—and left him sitting peacefully alone in his favourite chair in the middle of the library.

He wasn't sad and he wasn't in need of pity. He loved his garden, his knowledge of plants and the stars; he was utterly unsuitable for the throne, and there was no way she'd force him to do things that, in the end, people would laugh about.

Despite the way their relationship had started, she loved him as a brother, not as a husband. If it was too obvious that the infant girl was not his daughter . . . she'd deal with that later, but she couldn't see how that could ever be a certainty.

If he ever asked her about Li Fai, she would tell him the truth. No, she would not give him the opportunity to hear about it before she told him about Li Fai: that she needed to learn certain things about magic and that it might involve intimacy and that it didn't mean that she cared any less about looking after him.

Johanna shut the door with a soft snick, enclosing herself in the darkness of the hallway. The sound of raucous laughter drifted down the hall.

Back to the barbarians.

Johanna was late to the table. The food had already been brought, and the drinking had started. Faces were red from having been out in the open air all day, and it seemed that, in their way, the men were having a good time. King Benito had even enticed a serving maid to sit on his lap.

Duchess Carlotta met Johanna's gaze across the table, rolling her eyes. Johanna made a mental note to go down to

Francina when she could, and tell her about the things Li Fai had said about bringing up a child with magic.

Johanna was looking for a way to retire gracefully to her room when Anton came up from behind.

"Excuse me, Your Majesty. The guards have brought those weapons and arrested a man in relation to it. I'm sorry to disturb you."

"No, not at all. Where are the weapons?"

"In the Red Room. The prisoner is there, too. He has been asking for you, unsavoury character that he is."

"I'll see him now."

Johanna rose from the table. Father met her eyes across the room. He would know that something was up. Once again, she relied on him and Master Deim to keep the kings and dukes from attacking each other, although admittedly, most were far too drunk to do that.

She followed Anton into the foyer and into the corridor. Their footsteps echoed in the empty space.

There were two guards at the Red Room. One of them opened the door for her and Anton.

It was always very dark in this room, which reminded her of Baron Uti's castle: spooky and stale, imbued with the scent of long-gone history. Such rooms were whispered about in terms of who had been murdered there.

Another guard waited inside the room, next to the table on which stood a wooden crate. On the rug in front of the dark hearth lay a young man bound by his hands and feet. He wore dark but neat clothing, and she recognised the silver buckles on his boots. He lifted his head when Johanna came in, and she recognised that sleek ponytail and dark eyebrows. It was Sylvan, Duke Lothar's bandit son.

CHAPTER 18

JOHANNA SAT DOWN on the slightly musty couch. The guards faced her across the table where the crate stood. She noticed that one man had a bleeding scratch over his face and bruising around his eye. Apparently, Sylvan had put up a bit of a fight. She found the thought strangely amusing. Out of all the bandits that had captured her, she had respected Sylvan the most of all. He had not been like Sigvald, paying for his men to have their way with poor peasant girls.

"Tell me where and how you apprehended this man." And where was his bear?

"This bandit turned up at the Hemeldinck office, speaking in some foul language. We assumed he came to take delivery of the haul. We asked him why he was there and he said he had business with the Hemeldinck family. We asked him, did he know that they now consort with the enemy? And he said that anyone who fights against evil is no enemy of his. We asked him did he know that the Hemeldinck business was associated with the smuggling of arms, and he said that arms smuggling was better than peddling foul magic."

"Undo his bonds."

"But . . . Your Majesty . . ."

"Do as I say. I know this man. He is Sylvan, son of Duke Lothar of Gelre, and he's a strange character but no enemy of ours."

The guard did as Johanna ordered, still giving her uncertain looks.

That was the trouble with her. They didn't understand her because they didn't expect these sorts of commands. The Red Room was an audience chamber used for formal meetings, designed to keep the guests from getting too comfortable. It was also where, in the past, traitors were questioned and sometimes tortured, and where the king would have given orders to kill, raid and plunder.

Those practices had already stopped with King Nicholaos, since he had professed little interest in warfare and conquering. The conquering had, instead, been done in faraway lands by sea traders like the Nielands, and even most of that had been the conquering of trade.

Sylvan sat on the rug rubbing his wrists, rubbed raw by the rope. His face shone with sweat, and his cheeks were hollow, his eyes strangely bright.

"Have you had anything to eat?" Johanna asked.

His eyes widened, and she guessed not, so she ordered one of the guards to go to the kitchens and get a plate of food.

"Nothing too fancy?" the guard wanted to know.

"Whatever is left over. No one will miss it. And do hurry."

The man bowed and left the room.

Johanna shifted in the chair. The child was kicking her in the ribs.

"I heard that you and your husband took the throne," Sylvan said.

"After you delivered us to your father's castle, we were

reunited with our countrymen, escaped Florisheim and ousted Alexandre. It is a very long story."

"I'm sure equally long ballads will be written about it." Was that a tone of sarcasm?

It struck her how, while she trusted Sylvan more than the others, he had always been a loner and a character she completely failed to understand.

"What were you doing in Saardam?"

"My father tells me what to do."

"Picking up a delivery of illegal weapons from Florisheim? Does he tell you to do that? To be distributed where?"

"You don't understand anything."

"Try me."

He eyed one guard and then the other one. His lips twitched. Then he jerked his head. Despite the bad memories of that time that they were taken through the forest, Johanna still reacted to it. She understood his silent language. "Leave me alone with him."

"But, Your Majesty . . ."

"I know this man. He presents no danger." She hoped. Where *was* his bear?

The guards left the room, with reluctant expressions on their faces.

"I wish you'd listen to us," Anton said at the door. "This man is dangerous."

"I have listened. This is my decision."

He looked down. "I will be just outside the door."

"Understood."

Then Anton left, too, and the door shut.

Sylvan crawled backwards and pushed himself up on a chair. He was all knees and elbows to the point of being emaciated.

"I can see that life has not been good to you."

He snorted. "Somebody released a great number of ghosts

in our forest. We've been fighting the encroaching magic. We've lost most of the ground. It's coming this way."

Johanna nodded.

"You can fight magic with guns?"

"You can kill a magician with a lead bullet. You can't kill a magician with magic if that magician is stronger than you. That's where we went wrong previously."

"You mean the attempt to kill the baron at a dinner at his castle?"

"It was poison meant for my nephew."

"But someone told him it was there?"

He shook his head. "That glutton of an uncle of mine ate from the food and became ill. Then he assumed that it had been an attempt to kill him."

"That's why he jokes about it?"

Sylvan nodded. "My uncle knows what his son is up to. My uncle allowed that . . . shifter woman to marry him, with her strange daughter, because he thought she might be able to stop him."

By the Triune. "And what about Ignatius Hemeldinck?"

"He supports the baron. None of them were sure where you stood, because of your . . . child. I think the evil of the child does not twist the woman's mind."

"You're not sure then where *any* of the women stand."

"None that have children of the age of eight and younger."

In the shock of the revelations, she found some sanity in Li Fai's words. "Evil magic is not born. It is made through neglect and lack of schooling of children with magic."

He gave her a sharp look.

She continued, on very thin ice now, "You have a lot of magic, but your father loved you and taught you and you didn't turn bad. I have some magic, but my parents loved me. My mother knew what it was like to be an outcast, so she made sure I wasn't, even if she didn't know how to teach magic. Kylian was a child of an unfortunate union. He was probably hated from the day he was born."

"He was left on my uncle's doorstep. The Baron never seemed sure what to do with him, especially when he had tempers."

"There is a different kind of teaching." Johanna took her wooden box out of the purse. As soon as she opened the lid, the air whirled around it, became bright and formed into a tree.

Sylvan's eyes widened.

She told him what Li Fai had said about children with magic in the east, about teaching, about the mother touching them when they were born. "If we don't do this, we are going to have children go bad. I have already seen a boy who could easily take Kylian's place when he gets older. We need to get to him before his evil becomes irreversible."

Sylvan snorted. "That is all very well for later, but first we need to stop Kylian, and I very much doubt that he can be stopped with love and trinkets."

Blunt, but true.

"My father says that the magic lines have risen to the surface in Saardam, and that magic is fighting to sort out who will hold power over them and what the nature of this power will be."

She was going to say something, but the door opened and a servant maid came in with a tray. "You wanted this, Your Highness?"

"It's for him," Johanna said.

The maid put the tray on the table and backed away, wide eyed.

Sylvan grabbed a duck leg and tore at it with his teeth like a wild animal. Within a few short moments, it was reduced to bones.

It was kind of disturbing to watch. Feral. "How long since you've eaten?"

"Too long," he growled and stuffed half a sausage in his mouth and then wiped off the grease that ran down his chin.

"Where is your bear?"

An expression of pain went over his face and Johanna wished she hadn't asked. "He killed it. The monster killed it! I will not rest until I've killed him. This has been going on far too long. Waking ghosts, trying to raise people from the grave. I will kill him, if I have to do it with my bare hands!" He brought his fist down on the table with such force that the plate danced and the cider trembled in the glass.

Johanna shied away, reminded that he was not *quite* as harmless as she had pretended him to be. "So what about the guns? I have people here very upset because smugglers used their marks to illegally ship the weapons."

"Can't be helped. We need them."

"Who is *we*? The bandits?"

He laughed, not in a happy way. "Sigvald and his men are a bunch of idiots. They're only in it for the money. I needed them, they needed money, so that's where they stand. They do jobs for us, like bringing the guns. But lately they've been finding the overland route hard."

"But who in Saardam needs the guns and what for?"

"You're kidding? There will be a magical war the likes of which you have never seen before."

"A war? A fight, I believe that, but a war? You mean Kylian against the rest of us?"

"And his ghosts, and his *children*."

He looked at Johanna's stomach and a cold chill took hold of her.

Kylian's children.

"You have to get out of here, because it's that child he wants to complete his work."

Johanna was going to ask, "What work?" but she could put the facts together. She had seen Celine's ghost. She knew what he'd been trying to do. Despite what Sylvan said, she had a very strong suspicion that the bodies in the ice cellar were Kylian's victims waiting to be resurrected. Celine's body, having lain under the gravestone for two years before the king contacted Kylian, might not have been in any state to receive a ghost. He only needed another girl in the same family.

Bile rose in Johanna's throat. She desperately swallowed it away.

Sylvan sat back, having cleaned everything off his plate.

"Stay here in the palace," Johanna said. "You'll be protected by my guards and the presence of all my guests."

"Can't." And then, a bit later, "Can I have my guns back?"

Johanna reached for the crate. This one did not bear Li Han's stamp. It had a heavy lid with a metal latch. She undid it without touching the wood. Inside the crate, in a bed of straw, lay three powder guns with shining barrels and wooden handgrips. They were works of art, with little embellishing engravings in the metal and wood. The wooden handgrip had last been touched by an old man with a moustache, who had placed the guns next to each other as they still lay in a workshop that looked foreign to her.

True to Sylvan's word, it seemed that these guns had come from Florisheim.

"What are you going to do with them?"

He gave her a sideways look. "Friends are coming." It sounded evasive.

"I will leave the crate here," she said. "I will keep a guard on the door. If you can convince my arms advisor that you should have the guns, you can have them." She almost wished that she could be present at a meeting between Sylvan and Johan Delacoeur.

She called Anton in and told him to put Sylvan in a room

where he could be watched but that was not a prison cell. She told Sylvan that he needed to stay inside to avoid being arrested again. She figured he would find a way to get out anyway.

Johanna then went downstairs to see Francina and Natalya.

She found both women talking in the kitchen, where a fire burned in the hearth for heating water for bathing.

"Where is the infant?" she asked.

"He was asleep in the room," Francina said, her eyebrows raised.

"Don't leave him alone."

"He's not alone."

"Is there anyone else in the room?"

"No, but we're just next door."

"That's leaving him alone. Kylian is in town and he will be using his children. I don't know how and I don't know when. You have to hold your son and stroke him every day, and tell him that you love him, so that he can get used to your voice."

"But I already do that." She gave Johanna a deep frown. "What in the heaven's name is going on?"

"I wish I could tell you for certain."

JOHANNA LEFT THE TWO after having received assurances from Francina that she would do as Johanna asked.

In the foyer, she checked with Anton that Sylvan had been given a room, and was informed that he had.

The sound of raucous laughter drifted out the double doors into the hall. That was King William, arrogant and blissfully unaware that anything was happening.

Johanna couldn't bear the thought of having to go back inside that room. She hesitated in the foyer. Her belly ached and her back ached. She was tired enough to sleep, but couldn't bear the thought of lying flat in bed.

She went into the study and sat down in her chair. She was still not comfortable. The child squirmed, heartburn never ceased to bother her these days and her back was sore.

In the darkness, she eyed the piles of documents that she would have to deal with at the meeting tomorrow. This was the serious part of the meeting, where they got firm commitments from attendants and negotiated prices, locations and special considerations. That was where the attendants would put their money on the table. Did they want a cooperative facility in Saardam? That questions would be answered tomorrow.

Uncomfortable as she was, she must have dozed for a bit, because all of a sudden she woke up. It was pitch dark in the room, and she swore there had been a sound.

"Nellie?" Johanna attempted to say, but her tongue wouldn't cooperate.

There was no reply. But there had been a sound, she was sure of that.

Johanna stuffed her feet into her shoes and waddled to the door. The light was out in the hallway, and the window. The Moon peeked out between large clouds. The wan light silvered the lawn and Roald's vegetable garden, and the few hedges that had survived the fires and subsequent neglect and that Johanna insisted should be kept as mementos of Queen Cygna's old palace garden.

Beyond the garden wall, the water of the delta spread out. A slightly lighter strip on the horizon indicated where the moonlight reflected on the sand dunes.

A cloud slid in front of the Moon, casting palace garden in darkness, but patches of silvery light still tracked over the marshland on the other side of the river. There were also lighter patches in the water close by from the ghosts hanging around, waiting to pounce. Johanna counted at least eleven. An army of ghosts, waiting under the surface of the water.

She shivered. Maybe she should ask Li Fai to stay in the palace. What about Natalya? Maybe she should sleep upstairs? Just in case these ghosts came and attacked the palace. What had she said about spells? That the ghosts became used to their repelling power and that they lost effectiveness.

Johanna went to the bedroom where Roald was fast asleep. She gave him a shove so that he stopped snoring, but she couldn't get comfortable. Everything ached. She was too hot and when she threw the blankets off, she was cold. She lay awake until the first glimmer of daylight came into the room, when she couldn't stay in bed any longer.

Ow, ow, ow. Walking hurt her back. She awkwardly used the chamber pot, and even that hurt. Everything was stuck down there.

She wrestled herself into her dress and went in search of Nellie. She found her at the table with Frederik, chatting and laughing.

"Oh, mistress Johanna!" Nellie got up, abandoning her tea.

"Sit down." Johanna stumbled across the kitchen and dropped unceremoniously into a chair. She leaned back, closing her eyes. "Everything hurts, Nellie. I can't sleep anymore. I'm not ready to talk petty disagreements between self-important men."

Nellie put a cup of tea in front of her. "Oh, you can do everything. You've done worse things than this."

"Yes, but not while looking like a bloated pig's carcass."

"I do think your comparisons have become a little morbid, mistress Johanna."

"I *feel* morbid. I want this thing out of me."

"Well, your wish will soon come true." She put a plate with bread and jam in front of Johanna. "The meeting will be over, we'll ask Helena to come and give you some of her ointments and teas, you'll put your feet up, and wait."

"I'm through with waiting." And besides, there was a magical war left to fight. "Have you seen Sylvan?"

"What? He's here?" Nellie's eyes grew wide.

"He doesn't look very healthy, but yes. He says Kylian killed his bear and he's out for revenge."

"I don't like that man at all. Those were scary times."

Johanna nodded. They were.

Frederik rose and bowed. "I will be ready to protect you,

Your Majesty. I don't have much and I have no weapons training, but if necessary, I will fight."

"Thank you."

That was the story of Saardam: no shortage of people willing to act, but no one with the knowledge to do so.

Nellie got to work. A young girl came in, and Nellie ordered preparations for breakfast.

Johanna nibbled at the bread, but she felt ill and left half of it on the plate, certain that if she ate any more, she would throw up, and that would be embarrassing in the meeting.

She heaved herself to her feet and trundled off to her dressing room to get ready for the day. Nellie came in and helped her, informing her that the men were having breakfast, that all of them were there, and that most of them were in a talkative mood.

"That King Benito really is a piece of dirt," she said. "You know I don't like saying bad things about people, but do you know what he said to me?"

"I can guess the gist of it. Try to keep out of reach of his hands, and do your work. It will soon be quiet again." She met Nellie's eyes and burst into laughter. And Nellie laughed, too.

"You know, Nellie. I've told you this before, but you are my only and best friend. I don't know what I'd do without you."

"Don't say things like that, mistress Johanna. Look, you're making me cry." She wiped at her eyes.

Nellie left the room to check the laundry, and Johanna went into her study. She spread all her notes over the desk and sat down for a last-minute read-through, but she had trouble concentrating. The child was squirming and her insides were being battered.

Eventually, she gathered up her notes without having read anything and made her way to the meeting room sweaty, trembling and hoping that Father and Master Deim had their wits together, because she was certain her future held throwing up and having to retire to her room with a fever.

The meeting was held in the Red Room, where the servants had moved out the couches and chairs that normally stood there, and had replaced them with a table and straight-backed chairs. And, she was glad to see, the crate of smuggled guns was also gone.

Baron Uti and his party were already in the room. Johanna greeted them, seeing the baron in a new light. She was highly tempted to ask him some questions. From the moment of the fires, she had thought of the baron as supporting Kylian, but Sylvan had indicated that this might not be the case.

Fancy that. Even though they came from different angles, she and Baron Uti had been on the same side all along. The baron had just been too afraid of his son to let her know.

It was a good thing for the future of this agreement that would be negotiated today, but the entire agreement would be worthless if they couldn't also rein in Kylian's magic.

Johanna took her place at the table, gesturing for the baron and his party to do the same.

King Benito and his entourage came in, followed by King Leopold. Li Han entered with his wife. Johanna's heart jumped. Was there a reason Li Fai was not there? One by one, the others entered in quick succession.

Johanna opened the meeting with a brief welcome and handed it over to Father, who outlined the proposals and made it clear that this was the time for nations, families and businesses to make their commitments.

He ended with, "We are going ahead with this scheme. How big it will be will depend on the level of commitment we can get from your nations. It is our view that by implementing this plan, we can forestall future conflicts and enhance our region to place it on a competitive advantage in comparison with other trading regions. Let the discussions begin."

King William was the first to speak up. He put his elbows on the table and joined his fingers in a thoughtful gesture.

"How do we know that this plan, this plea for investment, is in fact not a grab for power in this region?"

King Benito was nodding and Duke Aroden sat with his arms crossed over his chest, looking belligerent.

Master Deim went on to explain that the developments and investments would deliver joint profits, and that a grab for power would look very different, with the benefits all channelled to one party.

King William argued, twisting arguments his way.

Baron Uti sat twiddling his thumbs, and his face grew redder and redder, until he slammed his hands on the table and said, "This is all very well, my friend, but if you're not interested, can you at least shut up and let those of us who do want to talk get a word in?"

King William whirled to him. "Who says I'm not interested?"

"Well. Are you? Because you might shut your trap for a moment if you are."

King William put both his hands on the table. "What did you say?"

"Gentlemen!" Johanna called out. Too loud and too angry, but she just couldn't stand it anymore.

King William gave one of his loud bellowing laughs. If it was possible, that irritated Johanna even more. It was as if something broke inside her.

"If you are not interested in this plan then there is the door. If the only response you can make when I, a woman of common birth, say something is to laugh, then there is the door. We are here as friends and colleagues, and we have the best interests of this region in mind. If you don't share that view, please, by all that's dear and by the Triune God whom you all profess to hate so much, get out of this room and leave!"

A stunned silence followed her words.

King William began, "Well, I—"

"You can go out there and face our real enemies. Out there is an army of magic, waiting for us to fail, waiting for us to become weak. They're cowards and hide. They use ghosts and apparitions that are incomplete resurrections. Their leader fancies himself a necromancer—" Someone gasped.

Johanna met Baron Uti's eyes.

"This man should have been stopped a long time ago. It suited most of you well enough that Alexandre occupied Saardam, because he would get rid of that hated church. The Church of the Triune is much older than you think and much stronger. They are not going to go away because the Belaman Church wants them gone. The harder you try to suppress them, the more they will resist. And it's irrelevant, because we're all on the same side. The Church of the Triune forbids magic, the Belaman Church allows some of it, but doesn't support magic used for evil either. None of us want to be overrun by evil magic. Magic manipulates royal houses. It penetrates their decisions and influences kings when they decide to go to war. Magic benefits by selling and making weapons. It benefits by creating discontent. We have seen this in all of your countries. It is now starting to happen in Saardam. We have to fight evil magic by standing together. We have to defeat the necromancer."

Another deep silence.

King William said again, "Well, I . . ." He spread his hands.

"Are you interested in contributing and helping us fight?"

"I don't know about that magic. I don't know that I would call it real—"

"Oh, it's real," the baron said.

"The necromancer is his son," King Leopold said.

"Thanks, cousin."

But King Leopold was far too serious to react to the snark. "It is serious. Magic spreads. It feeds on discontent and conflict. Can you imagine the ways it will use us to destroy each other once we figure out how to make iron ships?"

There were nods all around the table. Master Deim spread the pages of the agreement document over the smooth wooden surface. "Let's talk money."

Johanna leaned back. She was sweating and her stomach churned like crazy. Bile rose in her throat. By the Triune, this was not ending well. She rose.

All eyes were on her.

"I'm sorry, I have to . . . have a brief stop."

She rushed out of the room, through the hallway, and only just made the outhouse in time. Her stomach had been empty, and produced nothing more than a bit of slimy froth. Disgusting. Whoever had told her that the vomiting was restricted to the time before a woman knew she was with child was a huge liar.

She stood there, gulping air. She so desperately wanted to lie down and sleep, but she simply had to go back. But crossing the Red Room back to her seat, a hot pain stabbed through her lower belly. It wasn't bad enough to cry out, but by the Triune.

Johanna sat down, keeping her face straight, and drank some water while pretending to listen to the discussion between Master Deim and King Leopold. Pretending only. She heard nothing. The blood was roaring in her ears. The water went straight through her and she now needed to pee. When she wriggled on the seat, it felt like she had already had an accident. Her underdress felt wet. But the prospect of getting up to leave the room again was too embarrassing, so she stared at the documents, ignored all the conversation and concentrated on just breathing calmly.

Finally the men finished talking, and everyone was getting up from the table to move to the ballroom for the midday meal.

"Are you all right?" Father asked in a low voice when Johanna was the last to get up.

"I think so," she said, but by the Triune, she was not all right. Her dress was soaked and stuck to her backside. Even the chair seat felt damp. Luckily the heavy velvet overdress didn't show wetness.

"I just need to . . . I'll be along soon."

THE HALLWAY APPEARED to have grown tenfold in length, but she managed to make it to the bedroom. Nellie had been in to make the bed and open the curtains. Light streamed in through the window and she could see the chickens in the yard scratching for food. Roald would be out there somewhere. Some part of her wanted to call him. She wanted to admit that she wasn't well, that there was something wrong. But once she went down that path, the "weak woman" judgement was usually not far behind. And she absolutely had to be ready to get that agreement signed, and she had to fight Kylian.

First she needed to get rid of that wet dress. Standing in front of the mirror, she wrestled to undo the laces. The ends hung on her back and she could barely reach them. Where was Nellie?

She went to the corridor but didn't see her, but walking really hurt and she didn't dare venture down to the kitchens. She would leave a trail of puddles over the floor. She had just lost all control down there. A constant stream of drops trickled down her legs.

She twisted her arms around her back in front of the mirror and managed to reach the laces and pull them loose.

The back of the dress was wet. Her underdress was soaked. Even her stockings were wet. She wanted them off. She undid the tie at the top, but couldn't reach any further down, so she pulled the first one off by stepping on the toe and wriggling her foot out.

A breeze came into the open window and made her shiver. She felt ill and crampy. She had hardly eaten anything, but the meal appeared to have disagreed with her badly. She wriggled to other stocking off.

Ow, ow, ow.

She put the bedpan on the cabinet and sat on it. The touch of the cold rim to her skin made her shiver. But now matter how much effort she did, everything was so badly stuck down there, she couldn't even pee more than a few drops. Oh, this was terrible.

A cramp tore through her. Her jaws chattered. She badly needed to do a big one. The men were all at the midday meal talking about her but—oh, at least a big gush of fluid hit the pan.

Strangely, she felt nothing. It was impossible to see into the bedpan, she didn't think anything else had come out. The need increased.

She shivered and pushed. More fluid hit the pan.

Pushed again.

Oh. That actually hurt. Really badly. That's what you got when you couldn't go for so long. She should have eaten those plums that Nellie had mentioned.

Come on, come on.

Pushed again.

Her backside was so numb, she couldn't feel anything coming out.

It hurt. The pressure didn't let up. She needed to go. She

needed to get rid of this now. It had bothered her for days, and—

Ow.

Ow, ow. She couldn't stop pushing.

Oh, it hurt so much that it scared her. And somehow this seemed no ordinary business.

Wait—

She pushed herself off the bedpan. Her legs were trembling so much that they almost wouldn't support her weight. She grabbed the edge of the cabinet, hit the edge of the bedpan with her hand and sent it flying. It hit the ground with a big clang and bounced over the floor, spilling its contents everywhere.

Oh, by the Triune. She couldn't expect Nellie to clean that up. But she could barely move.

Johanna stood there, sweating and her legs trembling. Fluid ran down her legs. She looped her hand around her side and felt underneath. Her fingertips met tightly stretched slimy skin. There was something big and hard underneath.

"Oh, by the Triune, Nellie! Roald!"

The door remained closed.

"Anyone, help!"

She stood there with her legs wide, unable to move. The child's head pushed against the skin between her legs. Some fluid dribbled onto the floor. "Please, please Nellie! Get Helena!"

But it was far too late for all that.

A hot stab of pain went through Johanna's stomach. She couldn't restrain a cry. There was no way to stop it, no way to wait for Helena, or even to wait for anyone to turn up.

The underdress irritated her and she yanked it over her head and dropped it on the tiles. She held onto the cabinet to drop herself to one knee, and another knee, onto the fabric of the underdress. Moving was hard. Her breath came in shallow gasps.

She waited with her eyes closed until the pain and the need to push crested.

Johanna pushed, hunched over, her hand between her legs. The skin stretched.

It hurt, but it felt so good. She gasped a deep breath and pushed again. The skin parted under her hand and her fingertips met the slime-covered, hairy top of the infant's head. A flush of warmth went through her arm.

Magic.

She gasped for air again and pushed, groaning. Sweat ran down her forehead into her eyes.

The head was almost out. Oh, by the Triune, that hurt.

She was vaguely aware that the door to the room opened.

"Johanna!" Roald ran across the room and dropped to his knees next to her.

Another pain washed over her. Johanna pushed until she saw purple spots in her vision. Ow, ow, ow. She howled, and pushed. The child's head came out, waxy and covered in bloody slime. And the top of the body came out. Roald held his hand under the head so she wouldn't drop to the floor. And the rest of the body shot out with a gush of fluid. Roald caught her. A shrill cry filled the room.

"Oh!" Johanna cried, and she burst into tears.

Roald awkwardly cradled the screaming child in his arms. The fleshy cord was still attached to the disgusting mess of blood and tissue that lay on Johanna's underdress.

"Oh, mistress Johanna!" Nellie exclaimed from near the door. She ran across the room and threw a blanket over Johanna. "Let me help you into bed."

Nellie grabbed Johanna under the arms and hauled her up. Johanna almost fainted and then let herself be guided by

Nellie to the bed. "I'll call Helena immediately." And then she was gone.

Roald came to sit on the bed. He had grabbed the first thing out of the wardrobe—which happened to be a shirt—and wrapped it around the child. "It's a girl. See? It's a girl." He lifted up a corner of the fabric and pointed at the girl bits.

"Yes, Roald."

"Another of my women."

Johanna looked at the little face, scrunched up and covered in blood-streaked slime. The bottom lip trembled.

She felt dizzy. She felt . . . good. That had been surprisingly easy, nothing like the ordeal Greetje had gone through.

"Where did you even learn to help like that?"

"On the farm."

She held his hand. "I love you, Roald."

Nellie came back into the room, followed by Helena, who put her bag on the bed. "Oh, you didn't even wait for me."

She went on to tie the child's cord, and wash her, and wash Johanna.

Then someone knocked on the door. Nellie went to open. It was Father. His mouth was open. "I . . . I was going to say that the meeting was starting again. I guess you won't be able to make it."

"I'll be along later," Johanna said.

"Don't be silly," Nellie said.

"It's extremely important."

"You will take ten days' rest, as Helena will tell you."

Helena was nodding fervently.

"But farming women keep working straight away. I feel fine."

"You are no farmer's wife. I will make sure that the princess feeds properly before I leave."

Arguing with Helena seemed pointless. She did feel weak,

though, so she let Father take care of the meeting and let Nellie tuck her into bed.

Nellie took the little one from Johanna and cradled her in her arms. "What are you going to call her?"

"Celine," Roald said, and Johanna wanted to protest, because of that name. Because Celine's ghost was around, looking for a body to possess and because she didn't want the little infant girl with the dark eyes and the scrunched-up face to be that body.

A breeze went through the room and ruffled the curtains. It made the hair on Johanna's arms stand up. That was some construct of magic for sure. Kylian knew that the princess had been born.

She needed Loesie to come. She needed Natalya, Li Fai and Duke Lothar to ward off the ghosts.

But she couldn't make any valid arguments against using the name. To many people in Saardam, Celine was a saint, a beautiful young princess taken away from them by an illness.

Celine it was. She said softly, "Celine Sara Cygna."

As she watched, magic flared around the child. Already the light was turning golden. Kylian would come for her in the night. She needed to protect the little one by then.

Time was ticking.

Roald went back to the library, and Helena gave Johanna the child to feed. Her breasts were hard as stones, and as soon as the little one latched on, milk squirted out.

When the child was satisfied, Helena left, with a promise to come back later in the day.

"Please, Nellie, look after her well." Johanna slipped from the bed.

"Mistress, what are you doing?"

"I need to warn the kings. I need to find all the magicians in Saardam."

"You need to rest, mistress."

"Come on, Nellie, help me." She was bleeding, so she grabbed a towel, wadded it up and tied it between her legs with a strip of fabric. Her belly was floppy, the skin wrinkled. She put on her underdress.

Johanna went to the wardrobe. Eyed the corset. Guess now she didn't need to wear the special dress anymore. "Help me get this on."

"Mistress . . . Helena said . . ."

"I don't care what she said. This is more important than anything. Stay here with the child. Let no one into the room. Wait for me to come back."

CHAPTER 21

JOHANNA WALKED through the hallway to the Red Room not much later. She felt a little light-headed and the pad in her underwear already felt quite wet, but those were minor inconveniences. Oh, to be able to walk normally without feeling like a sea cow on land!

When she entered the room, she caught a snatch of discussion—it seemed to be about money—before everyone fell quiet. "I'm sorry for the delay."

King William sat opposite the door and was one of the first to see her. His mouth fell open while he stared at Johanna's normal dress. He called out, "Scandalous! You should be resting."

"There will be plenty of time to rest." Johanna gingerly sat on her chair. Ow, her backside was uncomfortable. She looked around the table. All of the faces were astonished except that of Li Fai's mother, who nodded, her lips pressed together.

Johanna went on. "Have you signed anything yet?"

"We were about to," Master Deim said.

"Well, we were talking about the payment terms," King

William said. "I'm not going to sign any document that includes unspecified terms that can be changed after signing to suit the provider of the service, in this case the Saardam Harbour Authority. I think—"

Johanna pulled a sheet of vellum out from the folder in front of her. "Why don't we sign first that we commit to the project, with terms to be hashed out later."

"Why?"

Father gave her a sharp look.

"If we sign this now, we have a commitment. We may need a second meeting. I hope we'll be able to hold that meeting tomorrow. For now, I'd like to get your commitment signed, and then I'd like you to return to your travel parties if they're in the palace. If they're not in the palace, I'd like you to bring those people into the palace for the night."

Several of the attendants made surprised noises.

"Why don't we finish the negotiations instead?" Duke Aroden asked.

"There is evil afoot in the city. Forces of magic are gathering in secret places and planning a move against us."

Baron Uti looked at her. He knew what this was about. He didn't protest, a sign of how badly she had misunderstood his position.

Johanna explained as quickly as possible all the things that had been going on.

King Benito banged his fist on the table when he spoke of Francina and the little red-haired boy. She even spoke about little Celine, not meeting Father's eyes while she did so.

She spoke of Loesie and her friend, Sylvan, and Duke Lothar whom she hadn't seen but who was said to be in town —and Baron Uti didn't once speak up. Then she explained about the ghosts, and for once the important men listened, because they had all seen Celine's ghost.

When she finished talking, they all protested at once.

King Leopold said that it couldn't be so bad, and that ghosts had never harmed anyone in Burovia, Estland and Gelre, where they were common. Several nobles of the King's Council still maintained that ghosts weren't real.

Johanna said, "This has been possible because none of us recognised the danger of magic. Instead of learning about it, we ignored it. We said it was part of the Belaman Church and sanctioned it. We made it the domain of priests, while most priests have absolutely no understanding of it. In Saardam, we ignored the issue of magic altogether."

"It must be forbidden forever!" Theo Kloostermans called out.

"No. We tried that, and it doesn't work. Children with magic are born every day. We must teach our children magic so that they can tell the proper ways of using it and the bad ways of using it. If we use magic for good, we will have our iron ships. Without using magic, we will forever be on the lookout for attacks by people who use magic, because there will always be more magicians than we can kill. We can trap them inside trees, and there will always be people who will free the evil because they believe it suits their aims."

Mayor of Saardam Joris DeCamp said, "But the spirit has been trapped in strong healthy wood. The tyrant had his soul crushed out of him when the tree grew."

"Yes, and someone has stolen a dagger from the Shepherd's house that may well be able to free the spirits from both trees."

"Stolen? Who still enters the Shepherd's house these days?"

"People who consort with evil. It was a young boy, possibly used by the necromancer to carry out his orders. No one suspects child magicians, and that is why he uses them, especially when the children already have magic and are unschooled in how to deal with it. All an evil man needs to do is offer them a treat or a trinket."

Baron Uti nodded, crossing his arms over his chest.

A deep silence followed Johanna's words.

Duke Aroden looked at her, wide-eyed. "So it's a war between spirits and ghosts, but what does all this have to do with us?"

Haven't you listened to a word I said? "It affects everyone. The necromancer wants to rule these lands through fear and magic. He's brought an army of ghosts. When we make agreements, it puts us in a stronger position. He doesn't want us to be strong. He wants us cowering from him and his magic. He wants the iron ships."

Li Han snorted. "We will never sell any of them."

Several people looked alarmed. It was the first time that Li Han had even commented on the existence of the ship.

He continued, "I will not get involved in fights. We are here to trade. We can easily go a place where all these troubles don't exist."

"But the lowlands are one of your biggest markets for silks and spices."

Li Han didn't reply to that. They both knew it was true. Li Han *could* go elsewhere, but apart from some of the towns around the Golden Sea, some of which would be hostile to him, no place had as many people with money living as close together as in the lowlands.

"We are now at an advantage. Last time, the necromancer burned the town and brought an army of lackeys with bears. We were unprepared and taken by surprise. This time we can see him coming. We have a number of people who can help us and all of us are on the same side."

"Well, I . . ." King William began in his usual belligerent tone.

"You are not on our side? Does Anglia have any magic?"

He snorted. Apparently not.

"Magic is spreading from the east. It will take us before it will take Anglia. It attempts to take control over our centres of trade, our churches and our places and means of travel. We know what they can do, if Alexandre's reign of terror is anything to go by. The palace is a safe zone. Call all your staff inside the palace if they aren't already here."

King William gave her a furtive, disturbed look. "You think so, huh?"

"I don't *think* so, I *know*. I can see the ghosts, I know what's going on east of here, I can see what they tried to do to our church, and what they're now doing to our children." She looked around the table to the collection of royal and noble faces.

Baron Uti sat nodding. His cousin King Leopold looked uneasy. King Benito glared at the baron. Duke Aroden's face was prim. Belonging to "the right side" of the Aroden family, he would have a profound dislike for magic and would consider anyone with magic "dirty".

Johanna took their silence as agreement.

Father quickly drafted up a statement that the kings and barons agreed on investing in the port facilities. Everyone signed it, including Johanna. Then the meeting dispersed. Johanna didn't know for sure that all the guests would indeed bring their travel parties into the palace, but at least she had tried.

She was extremely tired, her backside hurt, and she needed to get back to her little daughter. Altogether, the meeting had taken longer than she had expected, and her breasts were so hard with milk that even the press of the fabric of her dress on them was painful.

The sunlight came in low through the windows, but the light brought no warmth. By the Triune, it was as if all the joy had been sucked out of the air. She had better go back quickly—What were all these people doing there?

A veritable crowd had gathered in the hallway. They were servants of the palace and minor nobles of Saardam, those who had gathered in the foyer for the scraps of information that came out of the meeting.

They were all looking away from Johanna, to the end of the corridor where Nellie stood, holding Celine. Looking terrified.

Johanna could not normally see magic in the air, but the pulsing glow that radiated from Celine was so strong that even Johanna could see it. She bet even the nonmagical people could see it.

"Nellie!" Johanna pushed through the onlookers, who parted for her. She hesitated. There was an utterly evil look in Celine's little eyes, far too mature for a child of less than a day old.

"I don't know what to do, mistress Johanna." Nellie's eyes were wide with fear.

"Give her to me."

Johanna held out her hands. When Nellie put the bundle in Johanna's arms, magic swirled all around her. It crackled and stung her skin.

A woman gasped.

Someone whispered, "Sorcery!"

The magic found the wooden box in her purse. A strand of fire wound itself around the handles of the purse in ever-increasing speed. It whistled a high, screeching musical tone.

Johanna cradled the child against her chest, and put her hand over the box. The magic now swirled up her arm. She wriggled the box out of her purse with her free hand. She couldn't manage to open it with one hand, so she held the box out to Nellie. "Open it."

Nellie's terrified look fixed on the strands of magic. She took the box.

Johanna patted the child's back. The angry glow of magic vanished. But before Nellie could open the box, a man yelled, "Oh, look, look!" He pointed at the end of the corridor.

Johanna didn't want to look. She already knew that there were ghosts coming into the window, white ethereal presences oozing through the glass, shapeless patches of glowing ether that swirled and boiled. The window blew open, shattering glass. A larger, darker presence came in.

Johanna knew who this was, wearing his cloak of ghostly ether.

Several of the people behind her ran.

Johanna whispered, "Nellie, the box!"

Nellie whispered back, "It won't open!"

"Give it to me!"

But it was too late.

"Little Queen," said a male voice that sounded cultured and pleasant without being syrupy and strong without being overbearing.

She hadn't heard that voice since the fateful night on the Guentherite farm when . . . She tightened her arms about the child. Little Celine had calmed down. She was warm and sleepy. Not evil. *When a child is born with the art, it is neither good nor evil.*

Li Fai had said that. Where was he? Where was Roald? Where were Loesie and her friend, and Master Deim and Duke Lothar and Natalya and all the people who could help her? How could she get her box back?

The male voice went on, "You know why I am here."

"I don't recall inviting you."

"You invited all important persons in the lowlands. You didn't think to send a personal invitation to the most important one of all?"

He walked around her. Since she had seen him last, he'd grown a goatee. His red curls hung loose over his shoulders. The shimmering cloak made from ghost ether exuded a faint glow. Underneath, he wore black and his leather jerkin. He trailed a hand over her shoulder.

The chill that went through her body made her gasp. "Go away, Kylian."

He laughed. "Are you afraid of me?"

"No. I've just had enough of your games."

"You're not even a little bit afraid?" He leaned over her shoulder from behind, breathing cold air into her neck.

Johanna held her breath, determined not to flinch.

Celine squirmed in her arms, her little hands groping at Johanna's dress.

"Oh, look, the little one is hungry." He extended one finger to the child.

Johanna batted his hand away. "Keep your hands off her."

He laughed.

Celine started crying.

"I think she needs mother's milk, don't you?"

Johanna stroked Celine's head, desperate to show her love, desperate to protect her from Kylian. *What* was he up to?

"I think you'd like to feed her, wouldn't you? Answer me."

"I have no idea what you want. If you're so convinced that she needs feeding, then let me go so that I can feed her."

"Yes, she needs feeding. You need a quiet place to do that." His strong hand closed around her upper arm.

"Kylian, stop it!" Johanna tried to wrench herself loose, but the trick he'd taught her during their first meeting required two hands, and she only had one free hand.

He laughed. "You haven't forgotten anything."

He started off in the direction where the onlookers stood, dragging her with him. The servants and minor nobles and everyone else who had gathered there scurried out of the way.

A servant yelled out, "Leave our queen alone." He tried to pull Kylian's arm, but Kylian batted him away without even looking at the man.

In large strides, he dragged her through the hallway. Johanna had trouble keeping up with him, having given birth only at midday. He went into the ballroom, where the tables were ready for the evening meal, and out the double doors on the other side into the garden room.

Indeed, he took her to the place she feared: the bench that stood next to Celine's gravestone.

He pushed her down roughly. Celine was screaming, her toothless mouth wide open.

"Feed her."

"With you watching?"

"You think I don't know what a woman looks like?" But he turned around anyway, with the swish of his cloak.

Johanna undid the buttons at the front of her dress, opened it and pushed down her underdress. The fabric was wet with milk and her breast was so swollen that Celine found it hard to take the nipple. She screamed hysterically and nosed about, and the milk squirted in her face.

Kylian cleared his throat.

"Just go away!" Johanna shouted at him, feeling hot with frustration. "This is none of your business."

Celine found the nipple and latched onto her breast. Ouch. Quiet.

"But it is my business." He turned around. In his hand, palm up, he held the dagger with the bone and silver heft and the ruby pommel.

Johanna's heart jumped. "What are you doing with that thing?"

"You recognise it?" He smiled, not in a friendly way.

"Why should I recognise such a terrible ugly thing? It's a weapon. Put it away."

"As you wish, Your Majesty." His voice was mocking. He slipped the dagger in a sheath he carried on his belt. "You're a very bad liar, do you know that?"

Johanna did not respond. She covered Celine's little down-covered head with her hand. She thought of Li Fai's words, desperate to show Celine love before he could use her, because that was the reason he had come here, right?

She finished feeding on one breast and Johanna wriggled her around for the other one. She was so little, so vulnerable, so peaceful, now falling asleep in Johanna's arms.

Kylian came back within the pool of light cast by the lamp. He knelt on the gravestone, pulled that dreadful dagger out again, and traced the engraved letters in the headstone with the tip of the blade. "Come over here."

"Why?"

"Don't ask. Do as I say." He grabbed her upper arm and pulled her up. Celine woke up with a cry.

"See what you just did?"

"You can always give her to me."

"No way." Johanna cradled Celine against her chest. Her dress still hung open.

Kylian pulled her with him. She tried to resist, but his grip on her arm was like a vice. His nails dug into the soft skin under her arm.

He pulled her until she stood on top of the slab of stone that covered Princess Celine's grave.

"Stand here."

"No." She shifted aside and ducked his grasping hands, holding Celine close to her chest.

He grabbed her by the arm, squeezing the soft flesh in his hand. "Stupid woman, do as I say." He looked down the front of her dress, which she hadn't been able to close yet.

"No." She tried to twist her arm out of his grip, but he pulled her against him. He smelled of horse and leather. His breath was hot in her neck.

"Let's get this over and done with. You're getting to be very annoying. Give me the child."

"No. You're not having her for your foul tricks."

He laughed.

Then there was a sound at the door. Kylian look up sharply.

A male voice said. "Hey, you. Let go of *my* women."

Oh no, Roald.

CHAPTER 22

KYLIAN TURNED AROUND and laughed.

"Look who we have here. It's the lame prince."

"Watch what you're saying." Roald strode into the room.

Johanna shook her head, for all the effect that would have on him. He was in his formal clothes and had probably been getting ready for dinner.

He waved his hand at Kylian. "Come on, come on, let her go. I'm the king and you have to do as I say, or I will call the guards."

Kylian chuckled. "Do you know what I'll do to your guards?"

"They're my guards and they're the best. They will kill you."

Johanna continued shaking her head. If Roald annoyed him enough, Kylian would kill him without a thought, with that terrible magical dagger or simply with magic.

Roald took no notice of her. Kylian took no notice. They faced each other on top of the gravestone in the pool of light cast by the single oil lamp that always burned.

Roald was taller than Kylian, and all the work in the garden had done pleasing things to his physique.

"Look at you," Kylian sneered. "Do you really think you are someone? Do you think that you and your pathetic commoner fishwife can change the course of history and stop the march of real power across the land?"

"What are you talking about? You are here by yourself. I can see no power."

"Do you really think that I'm here alone?"

He snapped his fingers. The glass of one of the doors burst inwards. A slight figure carrying a pickaxe stepped into the room. Johanna recognised the young boy whom she had also seen in her visions.

She exclaimed, "Rue? Ruben?"

He turned to her with an ice-cold, detached look in his eyes. His face was pale as a ghost's. He was dressed in rags that were intended for a much bigger man, with the sleeves and legs rolled up.

"Rue, what has this evil man promised you in return for your help?"

The boy turned away, his face unemotional.

"I am your queen, this is your king. Answer me."

But he kept staring into the distance, white-knuckled hands holding onto the handle of his pickaxe.

Several other people had followed him into the room, stepping through the broken glass: a farmer whom Johanna had seen at the markets, two men in the uniforms of the city guards, and Octavio Nieland.

It was the sight of the latter that disturbed Johanna most. His face looked blank, his eyes empty, and he walked in a strange, jerky way. His chin, at least a few days unshaven, was wet and the drool ran down the front of his shirt . . . the same one he had worn to the dinner on the first night.

Behind those people came other . . . beings. A bear-like

animal that walked on its hind legs like a person, a tall and emaciated man with hollow eyes, scabbed lips and yellow teeth, who looked like he'd been dead yesterday and had been dug up from the grave.

Then there were the ghosts: so many of them, slipping in and out of human shapes, whirling, floating, oozing. All these people and beings gathered around where Kylian stood on the gravestone, a mass of magical, terrible creatures.

Kylian let go of Johanna's arm. She shuffled backwards off the gravestone, taking Roald with her. Maybe if Kylian was distracted, she would be able to reach the door to the ball room, but his terrible army spread around the room and covered all the exits. They were trapped.

Kylian raised his arms. His minions gathered around him and knelt on the ground, including Octavio Nieland, who, in his right mind, would never kneel to anybody. What had the necromancer done to him?

The ghosts formed the outer circle of the crowd, casting a broad ring of silver light.

Kylian started speaking. His words were harsh, sibilant, vibrating. They cut like shards of glass and hummed like a nest of angry hornets. His voice rasped like grating millstones and spat like demons.

The chant, this spell turned the air cold and radiated fear in rolling waves.

Johanna wanted to run, but the fear paralysed her. There was nowhere to run. This evil would take the entire city and all its citizens would be turned into jerky, mindless puppets like Octavio Nieland.

Roald had closed his arms around her and the child. Amazingly, Celine was fast asleep, her little fists balled against her cheeks.

Kylian's chanting grew louder and more frantic. The light from the oil lamp showed showers of spit flying from his mouth. Somewhere at the back of the crowd of beings, a voice started humming.

And then a female ghost floated in through the broken window, over the heads of the beings. It was Celine, in her yellow dress, barefoot, with snake-like tendrils of hair floating behind her as if she were underwater.

The humming grew louder until the air vibrated with it.

Roald tightened his grip around to Johanna's shoulders. His face was pale and sheened with sweat, his eyes wide.

The ghost came to a halt in front of Kylian. She held out her hands, opened her mouth and let out a low keening wail.

Kylian gestured to Johanna. "Bring her here."

Johanna held the child closer to her chest. Kylian's magic probed at her mind. She turned away, looking at the door, away from his demanding gaze.

Kylian repeated, "Bring her here."

"No," Johanna said. "She is only an infant. She has no fault and no business in your evil plans."

"She is mine!" Roald said.

Kylian laughed, not a pleasant sound. "This child has as much Carmine blood as your dear wife." His nostrils flared. A strand of magic flared out from him. It circled around Roald and pushed him aside. "Bring. Her. Here."

The magic spread to Johanna, swirling around her, binding her legs. She was forced to take a step forward, and another one. She couldn't stop and couldn't turn around. Her arms were frozen around the child, unable to release her, put her down or give her to Roald. He shouted at her, but she heard only Kylian's voice ordering her to come.

She came to him, the man whose seed had quickened in her stomach and who now demanded the fruit.

Celine's ghost stood before him, head bowed.

Kylian held his hands on top of each other against his

chest, holding the dagger with the bone and silver handle. The blade shimmered in the ghostly light.

Octavio Nieland rose from his subservient crouch and held out his hands. "Give her to me."

There was no way Johanna could disobey the command. She fought it with all her mind, but lost. Kylian's magic was too strong. Octavio took the swaddled child from her, and held the tiny infant out to Kylian—

Who raised the dagger—

Something inside Johanna's mind broke free of Kylian's magical stranglehold.

She screamed.

And there was a loud crash somewhere in the room, and the sound of many people running in, and the clashing of swords and whooshing of arrows.

The magical bonds fell away from Johanna's limbs.

A group of men had burst in through the door from the ballroom. Johanna spotted Johan Delacoeur, swinging his sword. He cut the head clean off one of Kylian's minions, but the man shambled after his head and put it back where it belonged.

"Sorcery, sorcery!" Another group of soldiers ran into the room, swinging burning torches through the ghosts, scattering shards of ether.

"Johanna, get out of here!" That was Father's voice.

But she couldn't run, not without Celine.

But Kylian and Octavio had disappeared in the chaos. The room was filled with a mixture of soldiers in glittering armour swinging swords or torches. The air was thick with smoke and ghost ether, punctured with moving spots of light from the torches. Swords clanged, men shouted. Beings wailed and growled.

Johanna screamed, "Octavio! Come here and give me the

princess if you dare." Her words got lost in the sounds of battle.

A shrill female voice cut through the noise, shouting harsh and guttural words.

That was Natalya, standing as a somewhat squat and dumpy silhouette against deep red light coming from the ballroom behind her. In response to Natalya's spell, many ghosts cleared the area around her. Johanna made her way to the door.

"He has Celine," she cried.

Duchess Carlotta was with Natalya, looking pale and wide-eyed.

Before Johanna could ask what the red light was, the source of it became visible through the smoke and mist: it was Li Fai's dragon, crouched on its haunches, radiating red light and breathing fire from its nostrils. It had grown to monstrous size, towering halfway to the ceiling of the ballroom.

Its owner stood next to it, with Master Deim.

They were accompanied by the shepherd, who protested loudly, "But I can't do that!"

"Enough," Master Deim said. "Our kingdom is in danger, our people, our very freedom. Are you going to be sanctimonious and still maintain that you know nothing about magic? We've all been hiding it, but none have been so stupid as you."

The shepherd was going to protest, but Master Deim spotted Johanna coming out of the garden room. He crossed the floor and enveloped her in a hug. "Oh, child, I thought you were lost."

"Please, he's got Celine!" Johanna's voice spilled over.

"Who has Celine? Where is Roald?"

"Kylian has her. He has Octavio Nieland and a whole lot of evil beings with him. Roald is in there as well. I couldn't see him anymore. Please we must do something or he will kill her."

A couple of the soldiers ran out of the room. They leaned, panting, against the wall next to the door, and unwound cloths and shirts from their faces.

They were not soldiers at all, but young women, farming women with strong arms and manlike physiques. These had to be the women from Loesie's farm. One of them carried a sword that was both rusty and blunt and looked far too heavy for her. Flashes of ghostly ether shimmered along the blade. She wore a man's clothing, and her face was dirty. Johanna met her eyes.

"Please, Your Majesty, don't go in there. It's a massacre in there," she said. "We can't fight them. There are too many and they're too strong. He has the dagger."

"He hasn't . . . used it yet?" Johanna felt sick.

"Oh no, the first thing he needs to do with it is cut the tree open that holds Alexandre's spirit. Then can perform his completely necromancy."

He was going join Celine's ghost with the infant Celine's body.

Johanna felt sick.

"The only way to fight him is to join the forces of nature," Li Fai said.

"You can't beat him," the woman said. "Believe me, many have tried."

"Have they tried at the same time?" Li Fai asked.

"What do you mean?"

"If we join all our magic together, we can each be one of the elements." He pointed at Master Deim and Johanna. "You can be water, you can be wood."

"But I don't have my box! Nellie has it." Panic washed over her.

"You will have the art of wood regardless of the box. You

have defended yourself with your art before you had the box, right?"

Yes, he was right, she had, but it was so long ago.

Li Fai went on, "I will have to be fire although it would be better to have a real fire artist here." Then he pointed at the shepherd. "And you must be air."

The shepherd gasped and protested, "I don't know how to—"

"Do you think any of us know?" said Master Deim. "We will do our best together. We get one chance at this, or we will all die. We need you. Rest assured we would gladly do without your whining if we could."

The shepherd stared at him, his face pale. Master Deim was one of the least excitable people Johanna knew, and for him to call the shepherd out for whining meant he had to be very angry.

The shepherd knew this. He let his shoulders sink. "I will try." He cast a suspicious look at the dragon.

Johanna would have loved to have Natalya and Loesie to draw on, but she had no idea where either of them were. Surely they would feel the magic in the air? What was Natalya's magic? What else did Loesie have other than wood magic?

Li Fai held out both his hands. She put her hand in his. His skin was warm and reminded her too uncomfortably of different time. One corner of his mouth moved up.

Master Deim took his other hand and then took hold of the shepherd, who still looked uncertain. The women soldiers followed close behind. Like this, they went into the garden room.

The oil light next to the grave had gone out. People and beasts struggled in the darkness, under a cloak of mist and smoke. The only thing Johanna could see was the moving light from torches and the pale glow from ghost ether. Weapons clanged, men screamed, ghosts keened.

They advanced into the room. The smell of steel, leather and burning flesh was strong. Johanna's foot hit something soft—it was the arm of a mangled body in a pool of blood.

Bile rose in her throat. If she survived this, she would raze this dreadful room of death to the ground.

Then: the shrill cry of an infant.

"Celine!"

Johanna wrenched her hand out of Li Fai's. She needed to save the child first, give her to someone to take her deep within the palace where Kylian could not reach her.

Kylian stood on top of the gravestone, holding Celine. Her shrill cry cut through the other noises: the groaning and whistling and hissing of sibilant voices. Shards of ghostly ether floated on the floor around his feet. The ground was covered in bodies and blood.

Johanna desperately wanted a weapon. She spotted the hilt of a sword sticking out from underneath a man's body. Was that Octavio Nieland? She felt sick.

No, a metal sword would be no good. Then she found something else: the pick axe that Rue had used to break the door. She picked it up, and wooden handle felt *alive* in her hands.

The glow from Li Fai's dragon lit the room from behind. So many dead bodies, not all of them human.

Kylian faced her, his eyes burning with anger. "You think you're an adept at magic now? You think you can defeat me?"

"Wood magic is stronger than fire magic and stronger than bear magic." Her hands gripped the handle of the pickaxe. She was so tired. She hoped that there would be no more walking or running involved, because she would surely faint.

"Maybe. But I've got the dagger of bone that can cut the spirits from the wood. I'll open the two ugly trees that you have wrought and free my disciples. Then I'll resurrect the princess' soul inside this little child and she will be mine."

"Why, Kylian? Whatever you do, you will never rule through fear. You can spread your seed all through the lowlands, but all that will achieve is that you will produce lots of other magicians, all of whom have different wishes and philosophies."

"The future lies in machines that can make things for us, using iron magic."

Li Han said, "If you want to be my father's partner in trade, spreading death is not the way to do it. We don't need you. There is a large mass of land across the Lamorian Ocean. We don't need to stay here or deal with you."

Then Master Deim asked in a mild voice, "I know that King Nicholaos paid you to resurrect Celine. But he's dead, you already have his money. Why are you so obsessed with her?"

Kylian stiffened. He stared at Master Deim, who came forward and pulled a roll of parchment out of his pocket. "Our dear queen wanted to know if there was any money left of the royal family's considerable fortunes, and I went to look for any investments and land ownership of assets that we could possibly sell. I came across this interesting piece of correspondence." He unrolled the parchment. "It says, 'Your eyes are as blue as the summer sky. Your hair fair as gold'—"

"Stop it!" Kylian shouted. His eyes bulged.

Master Deim coolly rolled the parchment back up and stuck it back in his pocket. "You get the idea. It's a letter from a love-struck adolescent to a young princess who was at the age of flowering into a woman, and who was struck by disease and died a little later. I couldn't find any evidence that the letter was ever responded to."

"Stop. It!" Kylian's nostrils flared.

"Master Deim, be careful," Johanna said. But, oh by the Triune, did he make a lot of sense.

Kylian had been love-struck with Celine when both were youngsters. She might have been promised to him and when she died unexpectedly, he'd been so bereft that he wanted to do everything to bring her back to life, to the point of turning into something too evil for words.

A child with the art is not born good or evil. It is the actions of men that make it so.

Those actions of men might have been nothing more than the baron scoffing at his son and telling him to get over it. She could totally see the baron doing that.

Kylian stared at Master Deim, trembling, his face shined with sweat, nostrils wide.

Master Deim held out his hands. "Give the child to me before worse things happen. This child is innocent, and true necromancy is probably impossible."

Johanna held her breath. Kylian closed his eyes and blew out a breath. Slowly, he handed the child to Master Deim.

"Now put down that dagger and come with me."

For a moment, it looked like Kylian would obey. Then he flinched.

"No. Never! I'll free my spirits and we'll rule the world with fear!"

He turned on his heel and made for the terrace doors.

"Call your power now!" Li Fai shouted. He took off after Kylian, who was already almost outside.

No, no. "Do something. Stop him." Johanna's voice broke into a squeal. She tried to run, but it felt like her insides would come out through her backside. She was unsteady on her feet. The wadded up towel felt wet with sticky blood. She was going to faint.

Master Deim ran to her and gave her the crying child. "Get to safety!"

Then he followed the shepherd and Li Fai into the garden, followed by the dragon in big bounding leaps.

A wall of water rose from the river and crashed into the garden. A whirlwind whipped it into a waterspout. The dragon breathed fire to boil the water. The steam formed into a giant whirlwind.

Kylian stopped at the empty spot where once there had been the fountain with the statue of the Triune. He flicked his hand. All the ghostly beings, the empty-faced people and other ghosts, bears and spirits shattered into thousands of pieces. He flicked his hand again, and the shards reformed into a cloak that grew over his body. He was drawing the magical power of all those beings inside him.

A male voice shouted, "Look over here you foul creature!"

Kylian looked. Everyone else in the garden looked, too.

Duke Lothar stood at the top of the stairs into the garden room. In his hands, he held a powder gun.

Kylian started laughing. "You think you can harm me with that thing?"

Duke Lothar lifted the gun. His hand tightened around the trigger. *Click.* Fire flashed.

Johanna covered her ears against the bang.

An unearthly voice rose from the apparition that Kylian had become. The terrible shrieking noise became louder and louder until her ears hurt. The magical being grew and grew until it had bloated to many times its size. Duke Lothar was busy with his gun, tamping in the powder, setting the trigger, putting in a bullet. . . . He held it up to Johanna. His lips moved. "Silver."

He aimed and fired at the bloated monstrosity. At this size, it was impossible for him to miss.

It exploded with a roar that shook the ground. Shards of magic flew outwards, into the sky, into the river, into the garden beds. They blew aside everyone in their way.

Johanna ducked behind a pillar.

Ghosts wailed and hissed as they sank into the river. The last Johanna saw was the ghost with the yellow dress and the flowing locks of hair. It lost shape as it hit the surface of the water, as the adolescent wishes of its owner died.

There was nothing left in the garden except a pile of smouldering ash.

CHAPTER 23

SILENCE.

Johanna came out from behind the pillar. The moon had risen and showed a scene of complete destruction. The entire side of the garden room was gone, even part of the roof of the ballroom had been blown off.

"Master Deim? Father? Li Fai?" Where was everyone?

A groan sounded behind her and someone said, "Keep your hands off *my* women."

Johanna whirled around. "Roald?"

He sat on his knees behind the next pillar. Johanna went to check on him. He said he had fallen and hurt his wrist, but he was otherwise fine.

Duke Lothar had gone to the remains of the fountain to check out his handiwork, poking the pile of ash with his feet. He found something on the ground and showed it to his son who had also come into the garden. It was the dagger with the bone hilt.

More people were coming out of the palace, stepping around the mess and carnage.

Johanna called, "Father?"

"Yes, I'm here." He was at the top of the stairs, just leaving the garden room.

"Thank the heavens you're fine."

Master Deim and the shepherd came stumbling out of the garden, both wet and covered in mud.

"Where is Li Fai?" She asked.

Master Deim shook his head. "I haven't seen him."

"Here, hold her." Johanna gave Celine to Father and went down the stairs into the garden. She stayed clear of the rubble and ash in the empty and broken fountain basin. She didn't want to see the awful sight of what was left of Kylian. When daylight came, the destruction would be clear enough.

The moonlight glittered on something in the garden bed. A large object lay there that was big enough to be a man.

"Li Fai?"

Yes, she was right, it was a body, but it was one of the palace guards. "Li Fai?" She found another body and another one further into the garden.

Then she recognised his boots on a body that lay face down in the grass.

No. Johanna crouched next to him.

"Li Fai!" Please, no. "Li Fai!" She shook his shoulder.

His box lay next to him, open, empty.

No. Where was the dragon? He *needed* his dragon.

She spotted a piece of tail from underneath a fallen section of roof to the side of the old fountain.

Johanna ran across the rubble-strewn lawn. She heaved off the beams and planks with all the strength she had. Roald joined to help her.

The dragon lay on its side. It had shrunk to the size of a dog and was fast fading. The red glow inside its body had almost disappeared.

She knelt, carefully slid her hands underneath and picked

it up. "Please, get better. Please." The tears streamed over her cheeks.

Johanna carried the dragon to Li Fai and put it on the grass next to the box. It opened an orange eye.

She took Li Fai's hand, which felt slack and cold, and nudged the dragon with her toes.

"Come on. Stop playing silly games with us. Get back in the box."

It lifted the tip of its tail, but didn't move.

Johanna picked up the box. She held it under the dragon's nose. It sniffed. Shivered. Then lay down its head and closed its eyes.

No, no, no.

Johanna clutched Li Fai's hand against her chest. With all her might, she thought about her happiness when she was with him. She thought about his kiss and how he had gently made love to her.

"Look, it's gone," Roald said.

The dragon had almost dissolved in the air. Johanna could barely see it through the haze of tears.

Johanna gathered the last wisps of ether in the box. She shut the lid and put it next to Li Fai's body.

"He's a good friend," Roald said.

You wouldn't know. Tears streamed over Johanna's face.

"Come." Master Deim pulled her up. "You've done far too much today. There is a lot of fixing up to be done tomorrow."

"I can't just leave him. Where are his parents?"

"I will tell them."

"Tell them that their only son is dead?"

"Johanna . . ."

"No, I will tell them. He is dead because of me."

"Please, calm down."

"I don't want to calm down. He died because he wanted to protect me."

Master Deim grabbed hold of both Johanna's wrists and looked her in the eyes. "Calm down. Remember, before you do anything silly, why Kylian upset all of the lowlands."

Because he'd fallen in love with Celine.

Because he didn't accept that she died.

Because he was a powerful untrained magician.

She understood the danger. She nodded, and pressed her lips together.

Master Deim breathed out.

Then there was a small sound behind them, a sharp intake of breath.

Johanna looked over her shoulder.

Li Fai's chest . . . was moving. She yanked herself out of Master Deim's grip and dropped to her knees. He was definitely breathing, coughing.

"Li Fai, Li Fai. Oh, help me get him inside!"

Together with Master Deim, she helped him up. He was quite a sight, completely soaked, his shirt sticking to his chest.

Li Fai coughed and Master Deim thumped his back.

Then he opened his eyes and looked at Johanna. He couldn't speak for the coughing, but the gratitude in his expression was enough.

A couple of guards moved Li Fai to the guest room. Johanna and Roald went to bed, and Johanna finally slept, interrupted only when Nellie came to bring Celine for feeding.

The next day showed the destruction of the ballroom and the garden room.

"We'll build another ball room on the other side of the palace," Johanna said. "The garden room can be a memorial garden." She would have memorials for Queen Cygna and King Nicholaos installed there.

The historic trade and investment agreement was signed

in the Red Room two days later and all around town, the town crier announced the news to cheers for Johanna and her father.

There would now be money for rebuilding the harbour and warehouses. Of course the kings, dukes and barons still bickered a lot before they signed it, and of course they didn't agree on everything, and of course the negotiations had been full of silly compromises and men behaving like toddlers.

Loesie and her girls left the next day. She wasn't interested in talk, she said when Johanna saw her, and there was work to be done. In winter when the children of the city couldn't play outdoors, Loesie would provide the first teachers of magic Saardam had ever seen.

The shepherd still didn't like it, but he knew better than to protest.

King William left two days later in his huge ship with billowing sails. Johanna stood by the window of her nursery in the palace, holding Celine, and watched the ship sail out the delta and out to sea.

Celine's little body glowed with magic. She would need a lot of training, but she would have a good teacher in Li Fai. She would be surrounded by loving people, and hopefully that would ward her off any bad paths that she might consider. As a magician, when she was grown and took the throne, she would protect Saardam.

Li Fai took a few months to recover fully, during which he moved to a small house with an office in East Harbour. His father and mother resumed the sea trade and came back with strange artefacts and stories of the large landmass on the other side of the Lamorian Ocean. They saw some strange people there, but most of all they spoke about the strange birds. Li Fai's mother's collection of drawings grew.

Life in Saardam became as close as it would ever be to normal.

Roald pottered in the garden, forgot to eat, hated meetings and never once wore his crown.

Houses were rebuilt, the harbour project started and flourished. Ships came in. Father took delivery of a new ship, appointed new crew, a new accountant and resumed the river trade.

Johanna continued to struggle with the King's Council and the old-fashioned men in it who grew only slightly less old-fashioned.

Celine learned to walk and run and kept Nellie busy. Her hair was straw-coloured and curly. She had freckles on her nose, and everyone commented how much she looked like Roald. Her magic made Johanna sure she *wasn't* Roald's, but it mattered little. Kylian was gone forever. The people of Saardam adored the princess.

In autumn of the next year, Johanna finally got to use the birthing chair for a very normal, hard and painful delivery where Helena could be present, water could be boiled and fires stoked in plenty of time.

But the story of the little black-haired, dark-eyed prince is one that might be told another day.

~

A Word of Thanks

THANK YOU for reading the Ghostspeaker Chronicles.

The story of Johanna's son is told in the Dragonspeaker Chronicles.

ABOUT THE AUTHOR

Patty Jansen lives in Sydney, Australia, where she spends most of her time writing Science Fiction and Fantasy.

Her story *This Peaceful State of War* placed first in the second quarter of the Writers of the Future contest and was published in their 27th anthology. She has also sold fiction to genre magazines such as Analog Science Fiction and Fact, Redstone SF and Aurealis.

Patty has written over twenty novels in both Science Fiction and Fantasy, including the *Icefire Trilogy* and the *Ambassador* series.

pattyjansen.com

BOOKS BY PATTY JANSEN

MORE INFORMATION:

PATTYJANSEN.COM